𝔄 Castle Christmas

Jimmy Bennett
2021

Library of Congress and Printing Information.

First Printing November 2021
Second Printing March 2024

Copyright © 2021 Jimmy Bennett
All Rights Reserved

In accordance with the United States Copyright Act, the scanning, uploading, and electronic sharing of any part of this book, ideas and concepts without the permission of the author or publisher constitute unlawful piracy and theft of the author's intellectual property. This includes movie productions, plays, written works, internet publications or any works produced and offered for free or for monetary exchange. Exceptions include brief quotations or excerpts for book reviews or articles in promotion of this publication. Special thanks from the author for supporting the writings of all authors and their works.

Printed in the United States of America

ISBN 978-0-998-1121-3-8

Dedication

To
Denise Marie Rippel

'For now I can only see your face when I close my eyes'

In August of 2020, my wife, Denise, was diagnosed with an aggressive form of cancer. She faced her poor prognosis with serenity and strength, mirroring the way she led her life- with pure common sense.

With that 'Swamp Yankee mentality', she forbade me to give her anything material that Christmas that would 'outlast me'. So, I tried to give her a moment, rather, a series of moments where she could escape into a world much gentler than the harsh reality we faced. I wrote this book for her. Denise loved romances and heart-warming, problem solving stories and I was over the moon when she told me she loved it. It was the last book she read.

I had no intentions of publishing this book. It was only intended for Denise and whatever special feelings it might have invoked in her. I told her this when she unwrapped it on Christmas morning.

Yet, after she read it, she asked me to share it when she was gone.

I hope you will enjoy it.

Jimmy Bennett

Author's Appreciation

'A Castle Christmas' could only be brought to life by a collaboration of friends and family, whom I have many to give thanks.

Thank you to my sister, Mary Ann, Kay Rippel, Jim Harris, and Chick and Sue Destefano for giving 'A Castle Christmas' it's first read. Not only did their kind words and praise spur me on, but they also helped immensely with early editing.

I would be remiss if I did not give a shout out to the 'Friends of Gillette Castle State Park' and Connecticut DEEP for their tireless efforts to keep Gillette's Castle, its history, and property in pristine shape for the world to enjoy. A special thanks to Paul Schiller, who narrates Gillette Castle videos with historical jewels of informational facts I weave into the story.

Thank you Toni-Lynn Miles for the many edits in preparation for the second printing in 2024.

Special thanks to Glen Rippel, my editor, publisher, graphic artist, and the driving force that brought this book to fruition. He has given life to my ideas and creates something tangible. I will be always grateful for his partnership and friendship.

Finally, a very special thanks to all my readers who support my work, spreading the word, and inspiring me to create more stories featuring William Gillette and Sherlock Holmes.

Thank you, Jimmy Bennett

Forward

This story, although completely fictitious, is loosely based on an urban legend. Gillette's Castle is a real location and is now a Connecticut State Park in East Haddam, Connecticut. William Gillette built the castle on a series of hills known as the Seven Sisters, high above the Connecticut River and moved into the castle in 1919. Later, he added a working scaled down railroad that wound its way around the property. His 144 foot yacht, the Aunt Polly, was berthed below the castle on the Connecticut River. The setting for this story is as true and as descriptive as possible.

Yukitaka Ozaki was William Gillette's faithful valet and companion for most of his life and others in the story are real historical figures, and some of the events are true to life. Yukitaka Ozaki's home is modest and still stands only a short walk from Gillette's Castle. Others, along with some characters and the way the situation unfolded, are purely out of my imagination.

Jimmy Bennett

A Castle Christmas

1

At a one-pump station at the side of Route One in Old Saybrook, on the Connecticut shoreline, the attendant carefully screwed the gas cap on the factory new 1922 Cadillac, then took a rag from his pocket and wiped his fingerprints off the chrome. He stepped back to admire the luxurious touring car, hand-built four months before. A soft clearing of the throat broke his reverie and he turned to see the driver of the car looking at him with a proud smile.

The man looked exactly right for the beautiful machine. Just over six feet tall with jet-black hair and bright blue eyes, his hand-tailored clothes were of the latest fashion and probably cost as much as the gas station would fetch if he had a mind to sell. He snapped out of his daydreaming and stepped up to the man.

"There you go, sir!" He looked a bit sheepish when he added, "I've got to charge you two dollars and twelve for the gas. She's got a big tank."

The man was amused and handed him a bill with Abe Lincoln..

"I'll get you change", the attendant said, hoping he had enough in the till to make up the difference.

The man flapped his hand, "Keep it."

The attendant was pleased but not surprised. This city slicker did not look like he would even bother with change. "Thank you much! Can I check your oil?"

The man shook his head. "No, Thanks. I topped it off this morning." His chauffeur gave the car a thorough going-over before they left New York City three hours before. "But the windscreen could use a rinse."

"Oh! Right away, sir." The attendant hustled over to the pump, next to a shack that served as the office, and filled a bucket with clean water. He added some soap powder and returned to the car. As he stepped on the running board to reach the center of the glass, the man tapped him gently on the shoulder. Pointing to the attendant's mid-section, he said, "Mind your buckle."

The man nodded and pulled out the front of his shirt over the buckle as he leaned into the car. As he wiped the road dust off the glass, he asked, "Mind if I ask where you folks are heading?"

"Just up the road a piece, to Had-Lyme. William Gillette's place. Know it?"

"Why sure! Everyone around here knows where the castle is! Can't miss it from the road or the river!"

The man laughed. "You have a point there!"

The castle was the most imposing structure on the Connecticut shoreline. Built of native granite stone, it sat on a series of hills known as the Seven Sisters, high above the Connecticut River. Wide at the base, the other three square stories were each a little smaller, giving it a less defensive look and more towards a fairy-tale, with extensive courtyards and walkways, all made of the same native stone. It was a park-like atmosphere.

The man who conceived, then had the castle built William Hooker Gillette, was larger in life than his home. A preeminent stage actor from 1885 to 1915, William was a great success in the theater business and not just for his acting, but also for his screen writing, set design, and sound and lighting innovations. He already had a supply of fame and fortune, when fate propelled him to a level far above anyone in show business had achieved since Wild Bill and his Wild West show.

While performing in London, his best friend and theater mogul, Charles Frohman, introduced him to Sir Arthur Conan Doyle and the two hit it off immediately. Doyle allowed him to bring his fictional detective, Sherlock Holmes, to the stage in any manner he wished.

Gillette brought the concept to America and wrote a few plays that caught on like wildfire. America could not get enough of the Sleuth on stage and William went on to write some more material and performed as Sherlock Holmes over a thousand times in the last fifteen years or so. He amassed enough wealth to build his dream home in a place where he could live quietly in his 'semi-retirement'. Nowadays, he lived a quiet life, rarely venturing out to tread the boards on stage.

The attendant moved around the front of the car to work on the passenger side glass and both men looked up when they heard a wooden spring door shut from behind the station. Moments later, a woman came around the corner, carefully stepping on the rocky path in her heels. Both men stopped to admire her beauty.

Average height, she wore a pale gray 'motoring suit' that molded to her curves from her slim legs and hips and over her ample bosom. Wisps of auburn hair peeked out over her forehead, from beneath her wide brimmed hat, which highlighted her brown eyes and soft features. Catherine Alexander was a well-put together dish.

Pulling on her gloves, she gave the attendant a smile as she walked around the front of the car. He moved toward the passenger side and opened the door for her with a dopey grin on his face. She gave him a dazzling smile and got into the car. The attendant picked up his bucket and got around to the driver's side, just as the man started the car. He stood looking into the car until the man rolled down the window.

The attendant lifted a hand and said, "Nice talking with you sir! You folks have a Merry Christmas!"

The driver smiled and dropped the car into gear. "You too, Bub." The woman echoed his sentiment and the car rolled onto the road and accelerated.

Catherine looked over with a sly smile on her face and said, "I see you made a new friend while I was using the outhouse."

He snorted. "Just making nice with the local yokels."

She swatted him playfully on the arm. "Don't be such a snob, Collin. 'Yokels' like him buy the tickets to your shows. Otherwise, you might have to work for a living."

Collin Frohman nearly missed the slot for the next gear at the remark. Sometimes, he was not sure if his girl was teasing or chiding him. True, it was folk like the attendant that bought the tickets at the theaters he owned or to the shows he produced, but he was not exactly one of the idle rich. Since the death of his father, Charles Frohman, a few years earlier, he had inherited the vast theater network known as the Syndicate. The Syndicate, along with a few lesser partners, controlled the theater business up and down the eastern seaboard and beyond. Collin's Syndicate even expanded into England – the homeland of Sir Conan Doyle and his Sherlock Holmes.

Collin's father, Charles Frohman had built the Syndicate from scratch with his blood, sweat, and tears, along with a stroke of good luck. Charles Frohman and William Gillette were very close friends and their rise to wealth and fame was side by side. Charles was the catalyst and with William's brilliance, they produced the Sherlock Holmes plays. So close were the two that Charles' children all called Gillette, 'Uncle Will'. William, for his part, adored Collin and his siblings and considered them as the children he never had. Especially Collin, who had spent a large part of his childhood in the ever-present company of his Uncle Will. Good parts of his summers growing up were spent on William's houseboat, the Aunt Polly, and in recent years, holidays, and business trips at the castle.

For the millionth time, Collin felt anger at the fact that his father hadn't been at the castle which he described as a 'great stone heap' - for the Christmas ceremony because he was murdered on the Lusitania. Collin had some grand times at the castle, where he found comfort with his uncle and much more.

Indeed, that was where he met the girl in the passenger seat. Catherine had been a maid in William's employ since shortly after he moved in. Hardworking, honest, and just sassy enough to make him laugh, Catherine had soon won over Gillette's heart, and he treated her like a daughter, though she still performed her duties in good swamp yankee fashion. It was not long before William asked her to move into the castle and gave her a room of her own. Even Ozaki, who was stern and reserved, warmed up to her. Mrs. Dana Woods, the cook and Catherine became as close as sisters despite their age difference.

Nature took its course over the many visits Collin had made to his 'Uncle's estate and the two were drawn together over time. What might have seemed most likely to some of Collin's upper crust friends and colleges was a romance with Catherine.. In a sense, she was the only good thing that came out of Charles Frohman's death.

Two months ago, after being intimate for nearly a year, they had married with an elaborate ceremony at Uncle Will's castle. Collin had brought her to his family estate in Yonkers, New York. He had spent the last months getting Catherine to know the city and introduced her into his society. He took her to all the finest restaurants, clubs, and, of course, the theater. Catherine was smart, funny, and beautiful and could hold her own with any of the society ladies. It did not hurt that his mother and sister had taken her under their wings. It was going grandly until he got a call from his uncle a few days prior.

He looked at her sideways, one eye on the road and said, "Honey, you know I'm just joking! There's no need to be jittery."

She reached over and squeezed his forearm. "I'm sorry dear. I'm just a little nervous about what we're walking into."

Collin sighed. "We've been over this a hundred times, dear." Exasperation seeping into his tone, "If there was a serious problem, he would have said and if he were ill, Ozaki or Dana would have contacted us! Like I keep telling you, it's just more of his melodramatics." He shrugged, "It can be irritating at times, but...that's what makes him who he is."

"I know, I know. However, you must admit, that was a strange summons-even for William!"

"I'll give you that." He admitted and replayed the telephone conversation in his head.

"Hello. Collin Frohman here."
"Collin! I'm surprised a man in your position would answer his own phone."
Collin laughed. "Only for you, Uncle Will! What do I owe this honor to? Please tell me you want to get back to work!"

"Not a chance, lad. Not even for my favorite nephew! I am relishing my retirement."

"You sure? You must have put your train to bed for the winter. You must be bored, puttering around that rock pile with Ozaki and Dana."

"Well, for one, the Seven Sister shoreline express is still running and will until the snow piles up too high to plow it off the tracks! As for the latter part of your statement, I will daresay I miss Catherine very much."

"Why? Is your little castle estate a mess?", Collin replied.

"Hardly. However, I will say that things ran smoother when she was here." He sighed theatrically and said, "Alas! Such are the fortunes of war and love! How is our Catherine?"

"She's great, Uncle. We are having the time of our lives."

There was a slight pause on the other end. "Yes, I'm sure you are."

When he said nothing more, Collin ventured, "How is everything out there in the boondocks?"

There was another pause. "Interesting, as of late. I'll tell you all about it when I see you."

Thinking that he was planning a visit to the city, Collin was excited. "When will that be? Are you planning to spend Christmas with us in New York? We would love to have you!"

The pause was more pronounced. "Actually, I was thinking the opposite. Collin, I need you and Catherine to come to Had-Lyme by next Monday. You may need to stay through Christmas. I know...I know you may find this intrusive and inconvenient, but I assure you it is necessary. Will you come?"

Collin was torn. This request dashed all his plans for the rest of the yule season and the plans he had for Catherine. Yet, something in his uncle's voice gave him concern.

"Could you, at least, tell me why this is so important?"

"No. If you don't come, there is no need for further discussion."

Collin let him sweat a minute, though he knew what his answer must be, and then replied in resignation. "Then I guess we'll be there Monday."

2

The road narrowed and twisted like a sheet in the wind as the new Caddy cruised up and down the hilly terrain. With the trees bared for winter, the river could be seen. Stillness was everywhere and only sheets of ice floating on the current showed any movement the calm water. After a steep incline, the road leveled off somewhat and Collin pointed off to their right.

"There she is!" he announced as a large shadow loomed in the distance. Partially obscured by the undulating land and the evergreen trees dotting the terrain, the castle was a blur of darkness against the grey sky. By the time they reached the driveway, only the top half of the castle was visible, yet it was enough to make Catherine sigh.

"You really missed the place, didn't you?" Collin observed as he turned onto the dirt road that led to the castle.

"Of course, I did!" She answered as if it was the most obvious thing in the world. Collin was pleased that she was happy, about returning to his Uncle's home.

After all, though she was more than a maid to his uncle, she still was not related by blood or marriage. She may have enjoyed working for William Gillette, but she was still working! Even though she had a room at the castle, her family home was just across the river. It is not as if she was some orphan William took off the streets!

In New York, Collin had introduced her to a life of wealth and position. Collin had tried to make her every dream of the big city come true, yet, she seemed more excited now than she had in the last two months.

Looking around as if she was seeing it for the first time, she suddenly grabbed his forearm and blurted, "Stop the car!"

Startled, Collin stood on the clutch and the brake and the Caddy's big Cooper tires skidded to a stop. He looked to Catheirne to see what the fuss was about, but she leaned up against him and pointed over her left shoulder.

"Look! He finished the bridge!"

Collin looked over to view a scene worthy of painting. In the depression of William's front lawn, he had expanded a standing pool of water into a small fishpond. Gracefully spanning the circle of water was an arched granite bridge that rivaled the bridges over the canals of Venice. With a blanket of unmarred snow surrounding the still dark water, the bridge was the perfect highlight for William Gillette's grand home.

Collin put his head down and kissed Catherine on the forehead. "Makes me want to take you for a stroll right now." Then he bumped her slightly with his shoulder and announced, "But we need to see a man about a horse!" He dropped the Caddy into gear and continued up the long meandering driveway.

Seconds later, they rounded a curve at the crest of the road and William Hooker Gillette's castle sprang into view in its entirety. Built with fitted stones rather than cut, with a great jagged wall atop the third level, it appeared rickety and if Collin did not know it was shored up by steel beams and gigantic oaken beams, he might have thought it on the verge of tumbling down. Darkened under the overcast sky, the massive structure was slightly ominous, with its odd angles and stone canopies over the windows that mirrored teeth of a mythical creature. The castle was surrounded by stone walkways and massive patios that were bare except for a thin dusting of snow. Collin braked and pulled over directly between a wooden footbridge straddling a depression that separated it from the castle. Across the drive, a door was set into the hill that was marked a 'Cold Storage'.

Collin got out of the car, while Catherine turned the rear-view mirror so she could check her hair and reapply lipstick after their long drive. She had been away from the household for months and she wanted to look her best. While she was carefully applying the lipstick, Collin said over his shoulder,

"Wonder where everyone is?"

Before he could reach into the car and beep the horn to alert the castle to their arrival, a voice rang out from the rear passenger side.

"Were you expecting a brass band perhaps?"

Startled, Collin whirled around with fists up and Catherine jumped as the lipstick traveled from her lips to her right ear. They both turned to see a small Asian man, holding a basket of vegetables and potatoes with a grin from ear to ear.

Collin lowered his hands and smiled. "Jesus Ozaki! I nearly wet myself."

Ozaki just grinned broader and opened the door for Catherine, who was hastily wiping a lipstick smear from her cheek. She stepped out of the car and threw her arms around him.

"It's good to see you, Mr. Ozaki!" Before she could say more, a female voice called out from the other side of the bridge.

"Hello you two! You made it!" The speaker was the cook, Mrs. Woods, and her shirt was billowing out as she hustled across the bridge to meet them. Catherine broke off from Ozaki and rushed around the trunk of the car to throw herself into Dana Woods' arms. While the girls hugged and greeted each other, Collin gave Ozaki a bow and a brief hug, and then they joined the women.

Dana Woods wet her thumb and reached over to wipe a smudge off that Catherine had missed. "What's this? Was your lipstick fighting back?"

Catherine scowled and cast an evil eye on Ozaki. "I almost got it in my eye when Mr. Ozaki appeared out of nowhere and scared the daylights out of us!"

Dana's eyes narrowed and she wagged a finger in Ozaki's face. "You little heathen! If I told you once-I have told you a thousand times! It's not polite to sneak up on people."

"I did no such thing!" he replied indignantly. "I was just getting the supplies you asked for when they pulled up. It's not my fault they were mooning at the house and not paying attention."

"Bull dinkers! You're worse than one of those damn cats and someday you'll get what you deserve for sneaking about!"

Ozaki scowled back at her and began to berate her with a stream of Japanese.

Dana put her hands on her hips and squared off in his tirade. "Don't you dare spit that gibberish at me, you..."

"Enough!" a loud voice called from the castle steps. "You will wake the hibernating bears!"

Everyone went silent. William Gillette, the lord of the castle, was slowly walking from the front doors. Tall, still handsome in his years, and more than debonair, he strode towards them with a smile that reflected a happy heart.

"Ah! The prodigal nephew and my wayward maid! I am so glad you came!"

As they hugged and greeted each other, Ozaki put his head down and darted back into the castle. Dana gave Catherine one more hug and squeezed Collin's arm, then looked at William. "I'll just go put lunch on the table."

Despite the great coat she wore, Catherine began to shiver in the biting wind off the river and William gallantly linked her arm in his and announced. "No need to catch our death of cold. Shall we go inside? We prepared a roaring fire to warm you both!"

Catherine nodded and they headed off. Collin turned back to the car.

"Where are you going?" William asked over his shoulder.

Collin shrugged, "You have the beautiful girl...I guess that leaves me with the luggage!"

"Leave them for now. Come along."

Once William closed the massive front doors behind them and William took Catherine's coat, Collin shrugged out of his coat and asked. "So, what's going on Uncle Will? Catherine and I have been on pins and needles since you called. Everything alright?"

William smiled and placed his reassuring hand on his shoulder. "I'm sorry if I had you concerned. Perhaps I should have worded my request better."

"Well, I was a little worried" Catherine asked. "What is this all about?"

William took her arm again and patted her hand. "Let's save that for after lunch. It's not my story to tell." He would say nothing more as they walked up the short stairway to the great room. The couple knew better than to try to pry it out of him before he was ready. They hurried up the dark stone stairway and through an over-sized intricately carved oak door into an open area.

The great room was the center of the keep. The size of a modest middle-class house, the lumpy rock walls were accented by great wooden beams and rattan mats. As Ozaki was not around to take their outer clothes, the couple walked across the room to the far wall and put their coats on a couch built into the rock under a balcony off the second-floor hallway.

Collin looked around to see what changes William had made in their absence. The player piano, the other curved couches built into some corners, and a sitting area with a small sofa, two easy chairs and a coffee table, and a corner table with chairs took up most of the available wall space as the room was expertly designed with hallways, doors, and staircases that led to otherparts of the castle. The only changes Collin could see was a new cat banner hanging down one wall and a gigantic fifteen-foot unadorned Christmas tree, across the room next to the fireplace.

Made from flat fieldstone six feet wide, the stonework climbed and got lost in the dim ceiling high above. Naturallyformed rocks looked like they were piled in an orderly fashion to frame the large fireplace that held a roaring fire. The fireplace was decorated with porcelain banjo playing frog figurines in the niches formed by the uneven stone with American pottery on the mantle, and a collection of South American artifacts on the left partially hidden by the tree.

In front of the fireplace was a thick wooden table that everyone called the 'cat' table because wooden balls hung down from the sides on leather strings that William's felines were fond of batting about. The table was ringed with five sturdy captain's chairs and set for a meal. Linen covered bowls and a silver tray in the center, beckoned the hungry travelers.

Dana appeared from the kitchen with another tray of food and Catherine instinctively went to help her. Dana stopped dead in her tracks and looked Catherine up and down.

"You look like quite the flapper in those clothes, Catherine!"

Catherine leaned over and whispered to her friend. "Honestly, I can't wait to get out of this rig and put on a regular dress, now that we're away from the city!" She pulled up the waist of her pants. "And these shoes are killing me!"

Dana gave her a sly smile and a wink. "That's the price you pay for big city fashion!"

Collin strolled over to join William, who was fussing with the table settings, while the girls whispered to each other.

"Gee, Uncle Will, I see your tree is still bare."

William glanced over at Ozaki and replied. "That too, will have to wait for a while."

Confused, Collin looked at Ozaki, who put his head down quickly and began to open bottles of soda pop and pour them over glasses of ice at each setting. Something was up. Collin could feel the tension in his uncle and his manservant, who both clammed up, yet he couldn't imagine what the elephant in the room was. He tried another tack.

"I see your still drinking your Coca-Cola."

"I'll say!" Dana exclaimed as she walked over with Catherine. "Now he's got the milk man bringing it once a week, by the case!"

William put on a haughty expression and took a long pull of the amber liquid. "A man needs some type of libation, now that we are in the throes of prohibition!"

Collin gasped and clutched his throat. "Don't tell me this place is dry now!"

William laughed and replied, "No need to panic, Collin. I still keep a full stock in its usual place." The usual place was a secret compartment in a hutch located in the lounge next to the dining area. With the right pushes on the correct panels, a false front opened to reveal a well-stocked array of the finest liquors. William was a law-abiding citizen, however he would never deny his guests no matter what the government may decree even though he was almost a teetotaler himself. "Your father would rise from his grave to chastise me, if I didn't."

Collin's face dropped and Catherine looked to him with concern, but Collin kept silent despite the remark.

William knew he had made a faux-paux and quickly tried to cover it up. "You may indulge yourself after we have had a discussion. Now, let's eat, so we can get down to business!"

Despite a fervent plea from Catherine, William would say no more, and they all sat down to eat. The conversation was light and easy, and soon they were talking as old friends, like they had never been apart. Soon their plates were cleared and pushed away.

"Sounds like you have had the time of your life, Catherine." Dana observed.

William gave the young couple a stern look. "I imagine they have, Mrs. Woods! Besides taking New York society by storm, Catherine has been learning to drive and attending Suffragette rallies!"

Catherine's jaw dropped and she blushed a vivid shade of crimson. She looked even more horrified when Dana remarked in a low voice, "Good for you, Girl!"

Collin was rocked for a moment but regained his composure quickly. He was not surprised that his uncle made an off the cuff observation like that- he was forever emulating his Sherlockian stage persona to surprise people. Collin knew about the rallies, but he felt poleaxed by the Catherine's driving license endeavors, which he knew nothing about! The look on Catherine's face confirmed he had hit the mark. He was not angry that she was learning to drive behind his back. In fact, he was looking forward to watching her squirm at the end of William's fishing line.

She managed to bait then hooked herself. "How could you possible know that?"

William waggled his eyebrows and laughed. "Child's play, my dear! I noticed the stains on your glove, light as they are, concentrated on the inside of the fingers and the palm of the right hand. Where one would grip a steering wheel and operate a shift. When you greeted me, I smelled the faint odor of walnuts..."

He turned to Collin, "I believe your chauffer, Bruno, is fond of using Walnut oil on the interior of your family's Lincoln Town car. Am I correct?"

Collin nodded and said to Catherine out of the side of his mouth. "We'll discuss this later, young lady." Then he squinted and added. "Then Bruno and I will have a talk!"

Catherine opened her mouth to protest, but William forestalled the argument. "Then there are the scuff marks on your shoes. They match Collin's perfectly...and everyone who works the pedals of an automobile."

There was silence while they took that in. Dana broke the lull. "Well! I'm impressed. Bravo, Mr. Sherlock Holmes!"

William smiled and nodded his head.

Dana gave Catherine a teasing look. "What tipped you off to the Suffragettes?"

Everyone held their breath and leaned forward to hear the revelation.

"Oh! That!" William said jovially, a wide grin on his face. "Collin's mother wrote me last week and mentioned you and Arianna attended the rally held by Miss Pankhurst."

"You don't oppose women getting the vote, do you Collin?" Dana asked, hoping to take some heat off her friend.

Collin snorted. "Of course not! You, Catherine, my mother, and Arianna have more sense than most of the men I know."

He looked sideways at Catherine. "But we're lucky these walls are thick when we discuss your driving-especially in the city!"

William grinned, "Actually, I'm putting you up on my boat, the Aunt Polly."

"We're not staying here in the castle?" Catherine asked, surprised.

William shrugged. "I hope you don't mind, but I'm sure you'll be comfortable. She's been warmed up and Ozaki stocked the larder for you." He smiled slyly, "You can have your discussions in private! I'm afraid there will be no room here at the house."

They glanced at William like he had three heads since the castle has multiple bedrooms.

"Which brings us to the business at hand. Collin, go fix yourself a drink and we will retire to the sitting area."

3

    Ozaki, silent this entire time, began to clear the dishes from the table, refusing to meet anyone's eyes as they rose and went to the sitting area. By the time they had settled, Collin returned with a cocktail and Ozaki had cleared the table with Dana's help. Collin settled on the couch between Catherine and Mrs. Woods and William took a chair next to a small table that held his pipe and tobacco. Ozaki stood at the edge of the area, head bowed.

    William took up his pipe and slowly filled the bowl. Placing it between his lips, he lit a match and puffed short shallow bursts until it was burning evenly. He took a long drag and blew an enormous cloud of bluish smoke that rose slowly into the endless ceiling.

    Collin shook his head and put his glass down on the table before him. Placing elbows on knees and clasping his hands in front of him, he said. "Alright, Uncle Will, that's enough suspense for one day."

    "Yes!" Dana chimed in. "What gives? The two of them," she waggled a finger between William and Ozaki, "have been acting strange this past week."

    William smiled ruefully and looked down at the smoldering pipe he held in his lap. "Yes...well...I suppose we have at that. But as I said before-it is not my story to tell." He popped his head up. "Though I will have a request after you have heard it." He looked over to his manservant and Ozaki sunk to his knees. Eyes cast to the floor in front of his knees, he said in a clear voice, filled with sorrow.

"I must beg your forgiveness. William's most of all, but I have wronged each of you three also." He lifted his head to look them in the eye. The anguish on his face cast a pall over the great room.

Dana, confused and sensitive, cried out, "Mr. Ozaki! What are you talking about? Get off the floor before you--"

William raised a finger and cut her off mid-sentence. He looked down on his valet with compassion and said gently, "Tell them everything, Ozaki. You owe them that."

Ozaki looked up at him and nodded. He squared his shoulders and began to tell them his deepest secret.

"You know me as Ozaki, and though that is my name, in part, my birth name was Yukitaka Ozaki. I was born in an ancient town of Japan, on the coast, that bears my family's name. I am descended from the Samurai and my family ruled the province of Ozaki for nearly two centuries before the Samurai class was abolished forty years ago. Still, my father is the ruler of Ozaki, though his title is worded differently. His word is life or death, and he is feared and respected in the Japanese parliament. He is an immensely powerful man and our family sits just below the emperor in the court of the Son of Heaven." Osaki paused and took a few breaths then continued.

"I, as eldest son, was groomed to inherit his position from birth. I was given the best education and training in the martial arts. I was privileged, strong, and a family confidant! One day, I committed an act of such sheer stupidity, my father had no choice but to turn me over to the authorities...or banish me from my home. By our customs, any punishment would bring more shame to my family, so I ended up stepping off a ship with thousands of other immigrants, dumped into New York City. I was lost, with little English and no prospects. My life of pampered privilege had done nothing to prepare me for a new life in America." He paused and looked up at his benefactor. "William took me into his service, helped me to speak your language properly, and taught me the strange customs of your society. Traveling with him, I saw many wonderful places, met many interesting people, and slowly made peace with my past mistakes." Osaki paused, reflecting on his past then continued.

"Over the years, I grew to realize that I preferred this freedom over the rigid and demanding life I had grown up with in Japan. I am happy to be alongside William and have grown to love my new family." He paused again and looked up at the three on the couch. Collin did not look too surprised, but Dana was startled by the admission and there were tears in Catherine's eyes.

"It was then I found the strength to finally communicate with my family back in Japan. Not to my father, of course. I was still bitter over my banishment, however I sent a letter to my brother, Yukio. He is my younger brother, and we were close as children. Though I had not seen or spoken to him for years, I have followed his achievements closely." Osaki paused and took a deep breath then continued.

"You see, my brother was everything my father wanted in a son, a man to carry on our family's influence. He is with the Government now, and, at one point, was the mayor of Tokyo. Recently, he presented your government with a gift of several hundred cherry trees that were planted throughout Washington D.C."

Collin whistled and exclaimed. "Wowser! I read about that! And he's your brother?"

Ozaki nodded his head slowly and wrung his hands a few times before he went on. "Of course, he was honored that I had kept track of him and wrote him after all these years. Yukio asked me how I had fared over the years. That is when it began.

"At first, my letters to Yukio had little exaggerations. I was doing well for myself, working in the theater business." He looked up at Collin, "I had listened to your father carp to William about the business for so many years, and I was quite familiar with its operations. So easy it was to write him that I was producing plays, opening new theaters, and building the Syndicate. As the years passed, I grew bolder and bolder with my pen; I made myself into a person of great wealth and prestige."

Collin's eyes went wide, and Ozaki nodded to him. "That's right. I put myself in your father's shoes...and claimed all his accomplishments as my own."

There was an uncomfortable silence for a moment. Ozaki looked to his employer. "I dug the hole I was in even deeper when I described the building of my new home—a great castle high above a beautiful river."

The women looked to William to see his reaction, but he only looked slightly amused. Collin kept his face like stone as he tried to balance the confession with his feelings. He was conflicted with the near reverent respect Osaki had for his father's memory and his love for his second 'uncle', who had been a mentor and friend for his entire life. Then Collin came to realize, he felt sorry for his uncle Osaki rather than harbored any anger. A question occurred to him.

"Uncle Ozaki, in the end, what does it matter? You are here and your family is in Japan. So, what if you...exaggerated some?"

Ozaki sighed and asked, "Do you remember your father's warning about boasting too much?"

Confused, Collin did not reply quickly, and Catherine put in. "He used to say, and I quote, 'Brag like an ass and it always comes back to bite you in the ass!'"

Ozaki dropped his head and reached into his jacket. He pulled out a letter and set it on the floor before his knees. "This is the teeth now imbedded in my rear end. My brother, Yukio, is currently in Washington D.C., on a diplomatic mission. Because the city is effectively shut down for the holidays, he has insisted on taking the train to see me. He wishes to see my new castle and celebrate my success." His eyes got a haunted look and he murmured as if he were alone. "My shame is unbearable."

In the awkward silence that followed, Dana shook her head and looked toward a panicked Collin. Catherine broke the quiet, in a compassionate voice. "Oh! Mr. Ozaki. We are so sorry. Is there any way we can help?"

As if on cue, William unlimbered himself to his feet and took a few steps before whirling to face them. "Actually...it is fortuitous that we are all here together!"

Collin instantly grew suspicious. The only reason they were here instead of celebrating in the city was because he summoned them! William smiled slyly and asked, "Is anyone familiar with the custom of Great Britain known as 'Boxing Day'?"

"YEESSS." Dana replied slowly, "Isn't that a day, somewhere around Christmas, when the servants and masters trade places for the day?"

Catherine caught right on. "You mean to switch places with Ozaki? Through the entire Yule time? Let his brother think he is the master, and you are the butler?" She shook her head. "You're a great actor Mr. Gillette, but I don't think even you could pull that off!"

"I could – only if I had help!"

Dana looked as if she swallowed a chicken bone and Catherine was dubious. Ozaki looked up at his boss, aghast, and shook his head violently, about to put the kibosh on the idea.

Collin spoke loudly and clearly. "We'll do it!"

William clapped his hands in glee and Ozaki was pole-axed as he seemed to sit a little straighter.

Collin looked at the girls. "We have to. Ozaki would do it for us!"

Catherine shrugged, and smiled, and though Dana was still uncertain, she reluctantly nodded.

Collin asked William, "So, how's this going to go and when is your brother due here?"

William answered sheepishly. "Actually, he won't be alone. Apparently, he will have his sister-in-law and her father with him. They will arrive by train in Chester at three, tomorrow afternoon.

Collin hung his head and chuckled, "This keeps getting better and better!"

William ignored the jibe. "That is why I am putting you and Catherine on my yacht, the Aunt Polly, to leave the guest rooms free."

Catherine quickly changed the subject. "Just what will our roles be in all this?"

"Mrs. Woods will keep her position as cook- of that, we have no choice! You Catherine, will resume your duties as our most efficient housekeeper, and Collin shall be the chauffeur, slash, houseboy. When he is not driving, he can help where he is needed. I, of course, shall be Mr. Ozaki's valet and butler. As I have observed the habits of the help around the world for nearly all my life, I shall mimic their every move...every nuance. This shall be my opus magnum. Even more special as I shall deny it to the public." He smiled benignly at them, "You, dear ones, are worthy of observing me!"

There was not much to say to that, and they sat in silence until a growl escaped Ozaki's lips. They all turned their attention to see him, eyes closed, lips pursed, and slowly shaking his head. His eyes snapped open, and he barked at Collin. "BAH! Why do you listen to this madman?" He swiveled his head to look up at William. "If he wants to act so badly- let him get back on the stage and make some money!" He turned back to Collin.

Before he could speak again, Collin shifted on the couch to face him and cut Osaki off. "It's a done deal, Uncle! We will show your family a good time, talk you up a little, and they get back on the train, happy, and none the wiser. Piece of cake."

Ozaki was not convinced. "This is my doing and I will face my shame with what little honor I have left. No. I can't spoil your Christmas."

Catherine leaned forward and tapped her ample chest, "Christmas is in the heart, Mr. Ozaki, just as you are in ours. If your Christmas is spoiled- all of ours will be spoiled! I admit it will be different," She beamed ear to ear, "I think it will be a hoot and a Christmas we will remember!"

Ozaki went to speak and this time Dana cut him off. "That's enough talk, Mr. Ozaki! Let's just get this done, so we can get back to normal."

This time, there was real moisture in Ozaki's eyes. "You are truly wonderful people...I am blessed." He let his forehead come to rest on the letter.

Dana tsk-tsked loudly and sprang to her feet. "Oh, get up! There will not be any of those heathen rites in our good Christian house!" She turned to William, who was smiling like the Cheshire cat and asked, "What's our plan William? And don't tell me you don't have one! I know you better than that."

He laughed. "Then I shall not disappoint! First, I think the children should get settled on the Aunt Polly. We can meet back here in an hour. We have a lot to do by three tomorrow!"

On the way out to the car, Catherine stopped at the side table to get her hat and gloves. She began to cast about the floor and surrounding area.

"What are you looking for, Catherine?" Collin asked.

Bewildered, she shrugged. "My other glove. I could have sworn I put them both here with my hat earlier."

4

Collin rode the brakes on the winding steep road to the riverbank. At the bottom, a left turn would take him past Ozaki's house and to the Had-Lyme ferry, which was the only way to cross the river for miles and a right took him to the dock where the Aunt Polly was berthed. The Polly was one-hundred and forty-four feet in length and over forty feet in the beam. She was seaworthy and had been sailed up and down the east coast, and William had made the Polly his home for the twenty years before he built the castle. The interior was lush with lavish staterooms and cabins, a salon, library, and a dining room. The bow was open with a canopy to ward off the elements and the stern had a large covered open sitting area. Collin knew her inside and out as he had sailed on her many times growing up.

Collin brought the Caddy to a gentle stop and switched off the motor. He smiled at Catherine, "The old girl looks great, doesn't she? William said she's fueled, stocked, and warmed up."

"Good," she replied. "This princess wants to freshen up before she turns back into a maid!"

Collin reached out with his right hand and took hers. "I'm sorry, Catherine. This is not the Christmas I had planned for us. We're going to miss a lot of great parties."

She snorted, "Don't apologize to me! Believe me, I'd much rather spend my Christmas helping a friend than going to those endless soirees with your boring society friends, who do nothing but try to out show each other! It will be nice to get back to the real world."

Collin was a bit miffed by her description of his friends and lifestyle. "Oh yes! Bowing and scraping to Ozaki and a group of strangers has always been a Christmas dream of mine!" He got out of the car and walked back to get the luggage before she saw an annoyance on his face.

Catherine got out her side and walked parallel to him. She leaned back when Collin opened the trunk and began to pull out their bags. "If you think this is such a bad idea, why did you agree so quickly?"

Collin shrugged and set the bags on the ground to shut the trunk. "Because it was a matter of life or death." He replied solemnly.

Catherine scrunched her face, "Now you're just being as melodramatic as your uncle! Telling his family the truth might be awkward and embarrassing, but it's hardly lethal!"

Collin stopped fussing with the luggage and straightened up to face her. Crossing his arms, he said in a serious tone. "Look, I grew up with Ozaki. He may seem like an eccentric butler to you, but I assure you, in his heart he is Japanese! He lectured me for hours on end about honor when I was younger – still does! And you can bet your last two bits that he meant it when he said, 'My shame will be unbearable'. Ten minutes after confessing to his brother, he would be dead by his own hand!"

Catherine's eyes popped out of her head, but one look at Collin's face convinced her he was not exaggerating. She reached down and pick up two of the bags. "Then we better get this right!" She walked past him towards the gangway on the stern of the yacht.

While the kids went to settle in and change on Polly, William remained at the sitting area and planned his next move. What he had proposed was nothing more than staging a play with a few people that were perfectly equipped to do that. Acting, directing, and set design was second nature to him. This would-be child's play to a professional.

He was actually looking forward to the challenge. It would be a role like no other he had ever played. No curtains, no breaks between scenes, and no crew to back him up. Fame and fortune he had gorged on, but this...this was acting in its purest form! It would be his opus-magnum, and not for applause. For his oldest and dearest friend, Osaki.

Dana and Catherine, he wasn't worried about. Both would simply resume their duties, doing what they always did and Collin, well, keeping him in line would be a challenge. Collin was much like his father, the bold Charles Frohman, William's thirty year business partner who he has fond thoughts.

Ozaki...well, Ozaki would have to be on his mark. Despite their many years together, William knew only what he had read about the Japanese culture and even less of Ozaki's family. He had no practical knowledge of how Ozaki should act. He could only hope Ozaki had picked up some working knowledge of the theater after being around it for nearly thirty years!

His mind turned to setting the stage when there was a loud series of knocks on the front door. William was still so deep in thought and assumed someone else would answer the door that he did not move at first. The second set of bangs set him into motion. He may as well get into character.

Mrs. Woods came from the kitchen hallway as William reached the stairs in the foyer. He looked at his cook and tapped his chest with his fingers. He would answer the door. Straightening his jack, he put a haughty expression on his face and slowly opened the door. To his surprise, it was the Chief Inspector from Chester, the town across the river, Kevin Rowan.

William's demeanor changed instantly. "Kevin! To what do I owe this pleasant surprise?" William had met the Chief Inspector when he first moved into the castle and had become good acquaintances.

Rowan looked as solemn as a pallbearer. "Afternoon, William."

"Come in, come, in!" William looked closely at the man and asked, "Is there a problem, Inspector? Are you here in an official capacity?"

Rowan stepped just inside the threshold, stopping with his back against the door. "No...well, that is to say, I thought I should be the one to bring it. Not in any official capacity...rather...well...just out of respect."

William smiled kindly, "You usually make more sense, Kevin. What did you bring me?"

"A telegram. The postmaster received it an hour ago and he called me. However, it is not for you, William. It's for Mrs. Woods. From the War Department."

A muffled gasp erupted from behind the door and made the Inspector jump. He slowly pushed the door open to reveal a trembling, teary eyed woman with an apron scrunched up in her fist and pressed against her lips.

Rowan was flustered and unsure of what to do or say. He wanted to give his condolences, because he knew, as Dana surely did, that a letter from the War Department was never good news. However, he did not want to offer sympathy before she had even read the letter. After a moment of silence, he simply held the letter out to her. That just upset her more. She shook her head quickly, still sniffling, she took a step backwards, putting her other hand behind her back. He was about the point out that her refusing the letter would not change its contents, but William saved him from further trauma.

"I'll take that Inspector." William reached out and took the dark yellow envelope from him. Dana seemed frozen with shock, so William flicked his eyes towards the outside and said, "I'll see that she reads it. Thank you for coming."

Rowan took the hint and nodded. He turned to Dana, tipped his hat and said, "Ma'am.", as he stepped out the door.

William stepped out behind him, closing the door. He looked at the letter again and sighed.

"Thank you for bringing this personally, Kevin. That was above the call of duty."

Rowan shrugged it off. "Poor woman. Won't be much of a Christmas for her, I guess. She'll need someone to help her through this. Guess its lucky Catherine and Collin are back for a visit."

Though the kids had been in town less than a few hours, William was not surprised that Rowan knew. Chief Inspector Rowan was a vigilant man.

Before William could reply, Rowan said, "Well, I should be going and you'd better see to your cook, William. I hope this doesn't spoil your Christmas as well."

William tapped the letter. "All we can do is hope, Inspector. After all, it is the season for miracles!"

When William went back inside, Dana was still standing in the same spot, but she seemed to have gotten some control back. Her face was smooth, and the apron hung down as it should, and her hands were folded at her waist. William took this for a good sign and held the letter out to her. Unfortunately, she was not ready. She shook her head and kept her hands to herself. William looked at her for a moment, and then stuck the letter in his jacket pocket.

He walked past her towards the kitchen and said as he passed her. "I would like a cup of tea, Mrs. Woods, if you please."

Instinctively, she followed him into the kitchen. He stopped next to a counter near the window and turned to face her. He said nothing but smiled and folded his hands behind his back. Calmer now, and somewhat embarrassed by her actions, she turned quickly to the stove. With military precision, she lit the stove and put the kettle on. She disappeared into the pantry and came back with a tray holding cups and a sugar bowl. She set the tray down and looked up at her employer.

"Open it."

Startled, William asked, "Excuse me?"

She sighed with exasperation. "Please open the letter and read it."

William slowly pulled the envelope from his pocket and asked her gently, "Shouldn't you be the one to open it?"

She did not answer; she just stared at him with tear-filled eyes. William sighed and took out his pocketknife. He carefully put the tip into the corner of the flap that sealed it and began to slowly work the blade across the top. He did not even make it halfway.

Mrs. Woods, with a viper's quickness, snatched the letter and tore it open. She let the envelope drift to the floor, and she shook out the telegram. Her eyes bulged, then narrowed, as she crammed the paper into her apron and leaped at William, throwing her arms around him and burying her face in his chest. It happened so fast that William barely had time to move the hand holding the knife to the side fearing he might harm his cook.

William was flummoxed, unsure of what the telegram stated, after all a telegram from the War Department was usually grim tidings. He knew her husband was a Navy officer and was currently serving in the Great War, though she rarely spoke of him.

He had grown close to Mrs. Woods over the years, but in a reserved way as fitting an employer and his employee that certainly never included her pressing her body tightly against his! He could feel every curve of her, and he didn't know whether to squat or wind his watch.

Mrs. Woods was a smart, attractive, and a straightforward woman. Traits that William admired. Holding her, he was surprised just how attractive she was. Afraid to speak and make matters worse, he patted her back gently until the worst of the sobbing was passed.

When she finally broke off and looked up at him, she had fury in her eyes.

"That...that...dirty...rotten...BASTARD!"

William's eyes flew open, and he stepped back quickly. Putting out his hands in a placating way, he stammered, "You mustn't blame the Inspector for bringing you the letter."

"Not him, you Ninny! John! My husband is the dirty rotten Bastard!"

William was not completely lost at her reaction. Anger was just one of the myriads of emotions a person felt at the loss of a spouse. He let her hold him quietly until her trembling eased.

She released him and stepped back, bringing up her apron to dry her eyes. "Forgive me, Mr. Gillette. I'm sure you don't need your cook acting like a hysterical schoolgirl!"

Certain that the telegram informed her that her husband was either dead, missing, or wounded, William was dying to know which, but it was against his nature to ask. When she did not volunteer more, he assured her, "Nonsense! You know you are much more than that to me! Now, you had quite a shock. Would you like me to have Collin take you home when he gets here?" Then he tried for a spot of levity. "Unless you'd like a chilly ride on my motorcycle?"

A small, hesitant smile came to her lips. "No, thank you very much! Not the way you fly around like a seagull with its tail on fire!"

She grew somber again. "I'm not sure I want to go to my house right now. There are just too many memories."

William was going to try to reassure her that everything would turn out fine, but even he did not have the words or the nerve to try. He had some experience with the pain she was feeling. A simpler idea came to him.

"Then don't go home! Stay here. You can have Catherine's old room. I know it's a bit small, but you would be comfortable." He was going to add that she should not spend the days of Christmas alone, andhe knew she was smart enough to know that.

She mulled it over, and then looked at him with a hint of suspicion. "You aren't just offering so I'll be on hand for your plan with Ozaki, are you?"

He smiled, "You and I both know that you would walk out on me right now if that was the case."

"You're damn right about that!" Then she gave a little laugh. "But what will people think?"

"Hah! Don't worry about that! By now, the whole town knows that Collin and Catherine are here for a visit." He suddenly took on the visage of an uppity Brit. "You shall be properly chaperoned, young lady."

She gave him a mock curtsy. "In that case, I accept." She gave him a serious look. "This is a very kind offer to a hysterical cook, Mr. Gillette."

This time, it was William that reached out and put his hands on her shoulders. "You have always been much more than 'cook'...and you know that."

She nodded and reached up to place her hands over his and squeezed. "Then I shall thank you for being a friend."

Oddly, William wasn't so sure that word covered it. He was beginning to see her in an entirely different light.

Before the conversation could continue, the sound of Collin's car came from the drive. Dana's eyes flickered to the door then she fixed her look on William. "Please, could we keep this between us for now? I do not want to explain things to the kids. There is enough going on."

William was afraid she might not be facing facts. "Catherine and Collin love you. They would want to support you now."

She shook her head. "I'll tell them when the time is right. I don't want to explain things to them yet."

'Hurt, gone, or dead', William thought to himself. What was there to explain? "I don't understand."

Down the stairs, the front door swung open, and Catherine called out a greeting.

Almost panicky, Dana pleaded with William, "I'll explain everything to you later, after dinner when everyone is gone."

Completely lost at sea, he nodded dumbly. "Of course, as you wish."

5

The couple clattered up the stairs and greeted William and Dana. Catherine was wearing a simple gray dress with sturdy work shoes. She had a apron from the Polly slung over her shoulder and she looked exactly as she did when she showed up for work in the year's past. Collin, on the other hand, was a completely different story.

Never had they seen him dressed so mundanely. Collin was a dedicated clotheshorse and his socks cost more than most men spend on a Sundays' best shirt. The plain woolen black pants fit him fine, as did the starched white shirt. The simple cut black jacket was a tad large, however it only made him seem more working class. He had a black, front brimmed hat under his arm and William was satisfied – until he looked down. The shoes he wore cost more than a chauffeur would make in six months. William stared at the shoes then raised his head and his eyebrows at Collin.

"What?" Collin huffed. "They're comfortable!"

"You'll wear the shoes I left you! Costume shows the character!" he reached over and put his hands-on Collin's shoulders. "Please! You must stay in character! Yukio Ozaki is not a stupid man! We will all need to be on our marks if we're to maintain this illusion!"

Collin sighed. "Alright, alright. I won't let you down, Uncle Will- or Ozaki!" He looked about the room. "Where is he anyways? I want to hear the script!"

"Ozaki is at his house. I sent him there with Ollie in the truck to pick up a few props we will need to set the stage. Ollie will bring the items up and Ozaki will stay at his house until dinnertime to prepare himself.

"Also, I don't want any of you to have personal contact with him until we're all comfortable with our parts. He cannot be chitchatting with us now and lording over us later. From now until his family leaves, we will all consider Ozaki the master of this house. So, the next time you lay eyes on him, treat him as such! He'll be far more convincing if he doesn't have to drop in and out of character!"

Dana looked uncertain. "Very well, as I agreed to this, Mr. Gillette..."

"AH!" William stopped her in mid-sentence. "First order of business. There will be no Misters and Sirs between us! We are all the staff. It's William, Collin, and Catherine." He smiled at his cook. "You, of course, shall remain Mrs. Woods. The chef needs a bit of special respect in a household."

She shook her head in amusement, "You're the director! But you tell Mr. Ozaki from me-Love him as we do, he can be...overbearing at times! Now, I'll treat him like a king, but if he rides herd on us, I'll see he spends this yuletide on the throne!"

They all laughed at the threat. Mrs. Woods threatened him every time he said a cross word to her, always claiming she would 'make him sleep through his birthday', or 'get the trots till next

Tuesday' with his next meal. It was a running gag in the household.

William grew serious. "You needn't worry about that! He won't treat you like an American head of the house would! He will treat you, as he knows his brother would expect. Japanese households are extremely structured. Ozaki will most likely only speak to me directly. He will pretend not to notice you three at all.

"But! If he does address you, it will only be to issue a command. Acknowledge him respectfully and carry out the task as quickly as possible, then disappear. Remember, I will always be nearby to run interference if there is a problem."

"What sort of problem are you thinking of?" Collin asked.

William looked down at him and sighed. "If I only knew there would be none to contend with. In any case, you girls know what to do, just go about your duties. Collin-you have been around servants your whole life! Just stifle the urge to be a wise apple and we'll pull this off."

He stopped and cocked an ear. "Ollie has arrived! Perfect!" He sent Collin and Catherine out to start unloading the props and he sided up to Dana and said, "I'll have Ollie take you home so you can get your things, and bring you back later." She nodded and got her coat.

Right after she went out, William went to the great room to wait for the first load. In minutes, Collin came staggering up the short staircase from the foyer, hefting a large, folded set of silkscreen panels. Catherine followed with some banners and a small statue.

He beamed ear to ear, "Come along, children. It's time to set the stage!"

The time flew by as they set the stage for their visitors. The job went much faster than anticipated because William and Ozaki had already removed most of William's personal items. A few Japanese screens were artfully placed. The wall hangings that depicted cats were replaced by banners that Ozaki had collected over the years. Every room, except for the kitchen, pantry, and dining room was subtly changed. In the study, William's effects were stowed away, and his playbills replaced with others from the business, signed to Ozaki. In the library, they placed a few oriental vases and some statuettes. Soon the ambiance changed. It was still a castle, but with a far east feel to it. Their last chore was to put Ozaki's Bon-Sai trees and his trimming table in the conservatory. Collin took the table first.

When he saw what was happening on the floor of the conservatory, he almost dropped the table. A fat orange and white cat was batting a frog across the stones, while dancing around it like a schoolyard bully. The frog lay on its back, blood dribbling from its mouth, and then the cat picked it up with its teeth and looked at Collin, as if to say "What?"

Collin had little experiences with cats and was too horrified to articulate, so he just yelled at the feline with a sound that was close to a bark.

The cat dropped the mouthful and shot past Collin's legs and out of the room. Collin could hear William and Catherine coming down the hall, so he set the table on its side and knelt next to the dead frog. He took his bandana out of his pocket and gently covered the amphibian, wondering how he was going to break the news to William.

Mike and Lena were a pair of frogs that William had kept in his conservatory since he had it built. They lived in the pool beneath the waterfall and William jokingly referred to them as his 'guard frogs'. He loved to tell the story of how they nearly gave my father the fright of his life when they jumped out of the pool one morning, right beside him. He was very fond of his pets and even kept a dish of dead flies and bugs to feed them close by. William would be crushed.

William walked in the door with Catherine at his heels. Both were holding a small Bon-Sai tree in a pot. William stopped and looked the scene over with a critical eye.

"I doubt that table will do us any good in that position, Collin. And what the blazes did you do to my cat?"

Collin, with a grave look on his face, sighed and walked up to his uncle.

"I have some bad news, Uncle Will. Awfully bad, I'm afraid. Something happened to Mike...or Lena, I'm not sure who."

William, trying to keep the smile off his face, handed the trees to Collin and went to the bandanna. He lifted one corner to expose his dead pet, then picked it up in the bandanna and walked it over to a wastebasket and dropped it in.

Collin said quickly, "I was too late to stop it! It was over before I walked into the room!"

William, seeing the concern on his face and his lips quivered, let the room be silent for moment. William shrugged. "No matter. It happens."

Collin was stunned by his blasé attitude. "You don't seem too broken up about it. I thought they were ...well, special to you!"

It was Catherine who burst out laughing first, and William could not hold back. Collin turned to her, irritated at her insensitivity, "What's so funny?"

She shook her head, still giggling. "Collin! They are frogs! And there are cats roaming everywhere. What do you expect would happen?"

Collin turned to William. "You mean...that wasn't Mike or Lena?"

"Well...yes and no." William explained. "This sort of thing happens every few months or so." He shrugged. "When it does, Ozaki or I just go down to the frog pond and catch another one. We simply name each one Mike or Lena.

"Though, I suppose, often we have two Mikes or two Lena's. Catherine might know the difference, but I surely don't. It doesn't matter really; I just like to have a pair."

Collin, feeling foolish, mumbled as he set the table upright. "There goes the myth of the 'Guard Frogs'!"

Catherine, still amused, put Osaki's Bon-Sai trees on the table and said to Collin. "I can't believe you thought they were the same frogs all these years. They do not last long in captivity, especially with cats around. Didn't you ever try to keep one when you were a kid?"

He shrugged. "There aren't a lot of amphibians in Yonkers." He smiled sheepishly, "I guess I overreacted when I saw that God damn cat swatting the poor little guy."

"There's no reason to blaspheme, Collin!" William said sharply. Being strong in faith, he was death on blaspheme.

"Bah!" Collin snapped back. "God did not care about that frog any more than he cared about my father!" With that, he stomped out of the room.

Catherine sighed, and then sighed again when she saw the hurt look on William's face. "I'm sorry, Mr. Gillette. Please don't be disappointed in him. He's still angry about his father's death."

"William," he said absently. "You must call me William. Mr. Gillette is put away for the time being. One slip like that could mar our efforts." He came back into focus. "Has Collin lost his faith? Does he blame God for his father's death?"

Catherine shrugged. "Not directly. He blames the U-boat captain specifically and the Germans in general, but I think he feels God was...indifferent. He has not been to church since Charles's funeral. Collin has said, 'When I asked him why, he said, my dad and I gave God his due our whole lives, and if that's how God wants to repay us...then the deal is off!'"

William shook his head slowly. "That just won't do, Catherine. He needs his faith-now more than ever!"

She gave him a stern look. "I wouldn't push him too hard about it, William. Unless you're willing to lose him. I already learned that for myself!"

It was nearly dark when Ozaki returned from his home. William greeted him at the door and took his hat and coat. Instead of his usual butler attire, Ozaki was wearing an expensive suit, with a silk robe of an oriental cut, over it. Collin and Catherine watched as William suggested that he take a quick tour of the castle so the new owner could see the changes they made. As they went from room to room, Ozaki became more and more assertive in his role. He made small changes, and then ordered William to assemble the staff. Collin and Catherine tried to keep the smile off their face as they stood at attention before him. When William asked him if everything was satisfactory, he replied, "It will do." Then he gave them all the stink eye, "But do not be lulled by my compliments. I expect supreme service while my brother is here!"

Before they could even react to that, the front door opened and Mrs. Woods came in. She joined them in the great room, and William relieved her of her coat and small suitcase. Seeing what was going on, she stood next to the couple, hands folded in front of her.

"Mrs. Woods will be staying here at the house, for the time being." William explained to Ozaki.

Collin and Catherine were obviously curious as the reason why. Mrs. Woods looked to her employer with pleading eyes. He quickly glossed things over. "The almanac is predicting a storm. It will be safer for her here. With your permission, sir!"

Ozaki snorted. "Of course! It would not do to have my cook floundering in the snow while my guest waited for their dinner!"

Mrs. Woods gave him a look, ignoring the remark. She looked to William and said, "Just let me get my things put away and I'll start on dinner. I still have enough time to make something special."

Usually, William ate at ten pm, but he shook his head slightly and flicked his eyes at Ozaki. The little man stepped and said haughtily to William, "Please tell the cook she has one hour. I will dine at eight o'clock. I think I will have a cocktail before dinner. Bring me a scotch and soda. I'll be in my study."

6

After Ozaki strutted off, William rolled his eyes and sent Dana off to the kitchen; delegating Collin to help her while Catherine took Dana's things up to her old room. William fetched his master his libation and returned to set the table for dinner. When Collin came out to tell him that the meal was ready, he noticed there was only one setting.

When he looked at his uncle, William raised an eyebrow at him. "You didn't think he was going to eat with the help, did you? There is a plate in the kitchen for us, old boy!"

Collin and Catherine were watching Dana artfully arranging food on a series of plates and carefully placing them on a large silver platter, then setting a dome over the top to keep it warm. William came in with a disgusted look on his face and began to open a dusty bottle.

"'The Master' wants champagne with dinner. One of my best bottles!"

The bell in the kitchen sounded. William had rigged it to summon Ozaki when he was needed. There was a secret button set in the floor at the head of the dining room table that operated it.

William sighed and piled the food and drink on a small waiter's cart which he wheeled out.

While the 'master' was eating, Mrs. Woods fixed a plate for Collin and Catherine, and they sat at the window counter to eat. William tried to join them, but every time he returned to the kitchen, the servant's bell would sound. It was nearly half an hour before he came in and sat at the counter with them. In between bites, he groused. "The master doesn't wish to be disturbed while he has an after dinner cigar." He rolled his eyes and lowered his voice. "Ozaki certainly took to his role, all right. You would think him Emperor of Japan if you didn't know him. If I had ever asked him to perform some of the services, he demanded of me – he'd have tossed me off the terrace!"

Collin winced. "Woo, boy! We may really be in for it. So, this is the English Boxing Day tradition?"

Mrs. Woods turned for the stove to face William. "Don't let this get out of hand, Mr. Gillette!"

William smiled at her. "No, no. As I explained to Catherine, you must call me William. You see..."

"Fine!" She cut him off and smiled sweetly at him. "Then you must call me Dana."

William leaned back in mock surprise. Then said thoughtfully, "Are you sure? According to Swamp Yankee customs, wouldn't that be too forward in the first five years of a relationship?" William had often teased her about her Swamp Yankee roots.

She smiled even wider. "You could have called me Dana after the first time I washed your underwear."

This sent the young couple into peals of laughter. William let them have their fun for a moment, and then said. "If you are finished, you two may retire to the Polly. Dana and I can handle it from here. I expect you both back here by six A.M. sharp."

Before they could answer, the servant bell rang again. He took the napkin off his lap and slapped it on the counter. Rising, he looked at the three and growled. "After this is all over, remind me to remove that damn bell!"

After he left the room, Collin and Catherine helped clean up the kitchen before they headed out. Dana was wiping out the sink when she asked, "Do you think we can really pull this off?"

Catherine answered. "I don't see why not. It isn't much different than when we had guests before. You just have to accept the switch in your head, and it should all seem natural."

Dana laughed. "You make it sound like changing your clothes. I'm not sure I can get used to calling Mr. Gillette, William!"

"Pshaw!" Catherine retorted. "The two of you act like an old married couple. You've been together long enough!"

She said it lightly, half in jest, but it resonated with Dana. After all, she had only seen her husband twice in the last three years, and she had been with William practically every day since.

When Collin and Catherine got to the Aunt Polly, he went directly below and started the engines. He spent much of his youth on the Polly and knew exactly where to set the idle so the engines would power the ship's systems. He checked the fuel and there was more than enough to keep them in lights and hot water for a few days. When he came up, he found Catherine undressing in the master suite.

"I'm heading for the shower!" she announced. "Between the road trip and discussions with William, I'm exhausted!"

"The water won't be hot for a half-hour or so." he warned her.

She scoffed and shook her head. "You didn't grow up with three brothers, parents and one bathroom! Cold showers are what I'm used to."

"Suit yourself, but I'm going to wait."

She slipped out of her undergarments and Collin waggled his eyebrows at her. "We could--" his eyes flickered to the bed, "occupy our time until the water warms up!"

Catherine snatched up a towel from the bed and wrapped it around her. She blew him a kiss as she headed into the bathroom. "I think you're the one who needs a cold shower!"

Realizing he would have to settle for the next best thing, he called through the door. "I'll be in the salon when you're finished!"

He was fixing his second drink when she came down the hall. Her hair was wrapped in a towel, and she wore a plain, but snug, nightgown. He pulled another glass from the rack and added a good measure of Scotch. Then he added seltzer and handed it to her.

"Oh my!" She said with a smile, "What are we drinking to?"

"The Yuletide, love and the season of cold showers and deceptions!"

Catherine raised hers in salute then slipped into another easy chair and curled her legs underneath her. She took a healthy swig and sighed with contentment.

Collin chuckled. "You are absolutely glowing my dear. The life of drudgery seems to suit you."

She stuck her tongue out at him. "Oh, don't be a snob! Honest work is good for the soul."

He flinched at that. "What? You don't think what I do is honest work?" Collin was defensive as he had been struggling to learn all the nuances of running a theater syndicate since his father passed away. Maybe he did not get grease under his fingernails, but it wasn't all three-martini lunches either!

"I didn't say that, but I've never seen you come home rumpled and sweaty after a day at the office! Besides, even if you never worked another day in your life, you would still have a hundred times more money that my entire family will make in the rest of their lives."

"Well, I can't help it if I was born into money. My father worked his butt off to make a good life for his family for generations! He started from nothing and built his fortune on blood, sweat, and tears!"

She took another pull on her drink and replied. "Which is why he appreciated his wealth in a way you could not!"

"I appreciate everything he did for me!" he snapped. "You enjoyed our time in New York, didn't you?"

"I enjoyed my time with you." she replied. "However, I am glad I am home now where I don't have to pretend." She rolled her eyes, "Imagine what that snooty crowd of yours would have whispered behind our backs if they found out I was a maid."

Collin stared at her crossly. The last thing he wanted was a fight, but her words hurt him. "I never asked you to pretend to be anything but the woman I love!...err...no, wait, that didn't sound right!" She laughed and he gathered himself. "I love you for who you are, and I'd break anyone who talked down to you!"

She sighed and drained her glass. "I know, Collin." She stood, careful to keep the towel around her head and stepped over to kiss him on the forehead. "And I love you for it. Look, it's been a long day and we are both tired. We need to get to bed."

He stood and put his arms around her. "Just let me wash up and I'll join you."

She looked up at him and smiled. "They'll be none of that, Bucko! We have to be up before dawn, and we need our sleep! Tomorrow is show time and we need to be sharp." She kissed him lightly to take the sting out of her words, then gave him the look and added, "And make that your last drink."

He sighed and made a puppy dog face, but she was not swayed. On either count.

Two hours passed since Osaki's dinner when William staggered into the kitchen looking like he had run a marathon. When she heard him approaching, Dana set aside the dough she had prepared for the next day's baking and went to fuss nervously at the stove. She should have been abed an hour ago, but she felt she owed William an explanation and had to wait for him to finish up for the evening. Still, she dreaded the conversation for many reasons.

William flapped a hand in greeting and flopped onto a stool at the counter, sagging as if his bones had melted. "Lord give me strength!"

"You still think we can pull this off? The guests haven't even arrived yet!"

"Of course, we can!" he replied confidently. "Though anything can go wrong. For instance--"

Dana cut him off, raising a spoon in her right hand over her shoulder. "Don't say it!" she barked in a loud whisper. Then she turned her head to show her profile and smiled. "Granny used to say- 'Let the devil hear your fears and he'll turn them into tears!'

William chuckled. "Wise woman. Does she have any advice about overbearing bosses? The little dictator will be the death of me!"

Dana gave him a sympathetic smile over her shoulder. "That bad?"

"You have no idea! My new master put me through the paces tonight. Ran me ragged, drawing his bath, setting out his clothes and every other menial task he could imagine! I don't know how valets do it!" He looked up at Dana and his expression brightened. "And you! How do you do it? It's late for you and you look fresh as a daisy!"

She turned around, holding a steaming mug in each hand. "This will help" she replied lifting the mugs up before setting them on the counter. She took a seat across from William and smiled. "And you needn't sweet talk me! I'm covered with flour and my hair's a mess!"

True, a few wisps had escaped her bun, but they only highlighted her fine facial features in William's eye. Shocked by the thought, he looked down at his mug and stammered. "What is this? A hot Toddy?"

"Better. Hot chocolate." She lifted the mug, blew across the top, and took a cautious sip. William followed suit and his eyes lit up.

"Oh! That's got a nice minty taste to it!" he took another sip and raised his eyebrows. "Dana! Schnapps!" he took another sip, "It's marvelous!"

"Thank you, kind sir. Catherine and I used to have one at the end of the day sometimes."

"I wish I had known. I would have joined you."

"That would have been nice." She said, "You know, it's funny, but we converse every day...but we never really sat down and talked. I mean, if it weren't for this charade, we might never have shared a cup of Dirty Heine." She laughed at the look on his face. "That's what Catherine and I named it. Dirty for the chocolate and 'heini' for the schnapps. We used to have one on the nights I stayed late."

William smiled. "Well, the name is somewhere between amusing and disgusting, yet I can see the attraction." He took another sip and sighed. "I always wondered what you girls were giggling about in here."

"Yet, you never came in." She looked down at the table, then back into his eyes. "Is that because I'm the help?"

William flinched and set his mug down hard enough to spill a little. "Good Heavens-No! It's just that...well, usually I am puttering around, busy with one project or another and I do travel still, though less and less as of late." He stopped making excuses and sighed. "And you are a married woman, Dana. I was afraid I might offend you if I was too familiar with you."

He added shyly. "I think this may be the first time we've ever been alone."

Dana's eyebrows went up. "You know, I think you're right! I never really thought about it." She smiled brightly, though it never reached her eyes. "I am glad we got this chance." She paused and drew in her breath to explain the telegram to William, but he cut her off, staring somewhere over her head with a faraway look in his eyes.

"Life is so strange at times." He smiled sadly at her. "You know, I too, know loss, Dana."

Compassion in her eyes, she asked softly. "Your speaking of your wife, Helen, aren't you?"

He nodded. "It was the hardest time in my life."

Softer still, she asked, "How did you deal with...the loss?"

Every fiber of William's body froze. He had not expected that question! That part of his life was buried deep in his heart, and he kept it there for the dread of a life without Helen still pained him greatly. However, the look of compassion in her eyes broke the walls between them that he had carefully built over the years, and he answered her honestly.

"Badly, I'm afraid. It took me nearly a year, recovering in a cabin in the Appalachian Mountains before I could even rejoin the world."

William saw the emotions on her face and went on, "That is the absolute truth. When Helen was taken from me, I didn't eat, drink, or sleep for so long, that I became so weak and ragged, and I contracted a serious illness. Not wanting the world to see my decline- I was a bit vain back then- I rented a cabin as far away from civilization I could find. I went there with the intention of dying." His face sagged and he lapsed into silence.

Dana reached out and put a hand on his forearm. "I'm sorry, William, I shouldn't have asked."

He put on a brave face, "No, No, Dana. It's alright. It was a long time ago..."

"So, what happened? You obviously didn't die."

He smiled at that. "Not for lack of trying, my dear! However...I guess that wasn't God's plan.

"Because, along with the cabin, I hired a housekeeper. An older negro woman, whom everyone called Aunt Polly."

"You named your yacht for her! I always wondered where you got that name! She must have made an impression on you."

"Oh! Yes, and much more. She tended to me, fed me, and bullied me back to health. If it weren't for her gentle care and old herbal remedies, I would have never made it. I still might not have, if she hadn't taught me a great lesson in life."

"What was that?"

"She taught me to put myself in God's hands. When I let him hold my grief, I began to live again."

"That's beautiful, William. You must have loved Helen very much."

"With a passion even the Bard could not expound on!" Then he smiled and reached over to pat her hand. "However, that was a long time ago. In time, I came to accept her passing."

They sat in silence for a moment, sipping their chocolate before Dana, with a coy look, asked, "And in all this time, did you ever consider remarrying?"

"No."

"Never? I'm surprised." she laughed, "I'm surprised some she devil hasn't sunk her claws in you! You're handsome, famous, and wealthy! Any woman would be happy to drag you down the aisle."

He laughed and fluttered his eyes, "You think I'm handsome?"

She swatted at him playfully. "I'm serious! You should have someone to share all this with."

"I do." He held up his hands and ticked off his fingers, "Ozaki, Collin, Catherine, and..." he looked her dead in the eye, "You."

Just then, one of the cats came racing through the kitchen with another hot on its tail. He laughed, "Oh, and six or is it seven, cats!"

She gave him a look, "You know what I mean."

He shrugged. "Truth be told, Dana, almost all the members of the fairer sex I encounter are connected to the theater in some way. I do not wish, and I never have, to bring my work home with me!"

Dana considered that for a moment and nodded. She grew thoughtful and William quietly concentrated on his mug until she was ready to say something. Finally, she took a swig from her mug and set it down.

"You are a kind man, William, and sweet for not asking...but I owe you an explanation for this afternoon." Her voice trailed off and she began to open the top buttons of her blouse.

William recoiled and turned his head away instinctively, averting his eyes. She snorted at his modesty and reached into her shirt to retrieve the telegram she received. She slid it across the table to him. He picked it up gingerly, all too aware, in the low gaslight, that she did not re-button her blouse.

"Are you sure?" he asked, then added, half-teasing, "Remember what Charlie used to say, 'Ask them nothing-tell them less!'"

She laughed, "Charles Frohman said a lot of things. Read it...please. Besides, I need to talk to somebody, and you already know...that I received it."

"If you're sure," William replied as he opened the envelope. He read the two lines of the message and his eyes widen to saucers. He looked up and lowered the page. "I am so sorry, Dana."

He set the paper between them, and his eyes drifted over the short, but severe note again,

'Dana. Need the divorce as soon as possible. Have met someone. Papers to follow...John.'

William's first thought was relief that the man was alive, but after digesting the message he was not sure if that would have been better news to Dana.

"I'm sorry, Dana. I know it's not what you wanted."

"Why do you say that?"

He shrugged. "Perhaps it was because you called him a dirty rotten bastard when you read it this afternoon."

She scoffed. "It wasn't about the ...request! I was angry the slimy toad got it put in an official War Department telegram so I would be sure to get it!"

"Ah!" William said thoughtfully. "And you were incensed so many other people would have seen the message."

She nodded fiercely. "Just so!"

"Well, I wouldn't fret so. The few people who send and receive telegrams are usually quite discreet". He paused and added, "I don't know what to say about your husband. I am not impressed by the cavalier way he broke the news to you. Yet, I hardly knew the man. I believe I met him just once."

"You're lucky." She replied calmly.

William shook his head, as if he misheard her. "Pardon me, did you say"--

She answered before he could finish the question. "You're lucky you never had to associate with that son of a bitch! He was a bully and a coward."

As he just read a missive stating the opposite, he could not reconcile with her last accusation.

"Coward? Why do you brand him a coward?"

"What else do you call a woman beater?"

William's eyes flashed and narrowed until his eyebrows met. He abhorred the practice of women beating. He found it cruel, demeaning, and considered it a mortal sin. An overwhelming desire to protect her welled inside him.

"I see." He said grimly, then fell silent. Confusion was breaking his anger apart, as he could not read her feelings on the matter.

She smiled sadly and sighed. "I suppose I should explain myself."

"Only if you want to, Dana."

She looked him squarely in the eye. "I do. Only one other person knows this story and he doesn't know it all."

William's curiosity was peaked, but she started without naming him.

"I met John when he was a young Navy ensign. He assisted in the building of the new submarine base in Groton. After it was up and running, he was assigned to a submarine, where I assumed, he still be stationed or until he got himself killed.

The first few years, it was the typical love story. We fell in love and married. He had shore duty and we had our little place on the river. They were good years. Then he was gone for longer and longer periods of time. By the sixth or seventh year, he was home only four weeks a year. I could give you a lot of reasons, excuses, or accusations, but the truth was we couldn't sustain our love being together only four weeks a year."

"And so, you started fighting?"

She thought about it. "Not fighting so much, more like we started acting like strangers. Inevitably, whenever John was home, he would ...get rough with me-especially if he were drinking. Usually I could lock myself in the spare bedroom and he would apologize the next day. Then, one day it went too far. John was given a promotion to Lieutenant, and the boat he was assigned to was stationed in Virginia. He told me to get dressed for the ceremony and in the same breath, told me we were relocating! I told him, in no uncertain terms, that I was not going anywhere and if he wanted that promotion, he could slink away down south on his own. I reminded him that, as little as he was home, I would hardly notice. I told him he could go to his ceremony stag and I locked myself in the bedroom. He stormed out and I spent hours trying to find a way to tell him we had to resolve our differences. I knew he would never give me a divorce, so we had to come to some kind of agreement. When he came home, late that night, I came out to talk to him. That was a bad mistake. He had been drinking heavily and he was full of pride and fury. Proud of his new rank and furious at me! He cursed me for embarrassing him in front of the other officers by not attending and he told me I was moving to Norfolk-like it or not!" Dana paused, took a few deep breaths, and continued.

"I lost my temper and told him to go jump in the river. Something snapped inside him and he ... well, he hit and kicked me until I blacked out. I...I thought I going to die." No tears slid down her cheeks, however her eyes were moist as she paused and sipped her drink. After a moment, she sighed and brushed at her eyes with a napkin.

"I woke up after a few hours. John was passed out in a chair. I slipped past him and went out the door. I...I was in rough shape and could hardly walk. I made it to the road and started stumbling towards town. I did not know how far I made it- or even knew where I was going for that matter- when I collapsed. If a young constable hadn't come across me, on his way home, I may have lain there until I died. When he helped me up, he saw the bruises on my face and pried the story out of me."

"I hope you had that scoundrel arrested then!"

She shook her head slowly. "No."

"Why not?"

She gave him a level look. "Because it's a man's world! He was an officer in the United States Navy and I was a disobedient wife! We both knew it would likely go badly for me if it were made public."

She gave William a withering look. "How would that stack up against the 'rule of thumb'!"

William was confused. "I am not familiar with the expression, 'Rule of thumb.'"

She grimaced. "It's a law that states a man cannot beat his wife with a stick that is any thicker than his thumb."

"That is monstrous! What blithering idiot came up with that?"

Dana snorted. "A male one."

"So, what happened?"

She managed to smile. "That young officer walked me back to the house. To John's credit, he had packed all his things into his car by then and was about to leave. He tried to talk to me, but I limped right past him and into the house, leaving him with the constable.

"When I got inside, I peeked out through the curtains. I did not know what the policeman was saying, but he pulled his revolver from his belt and stuck it right between John's eyes. He held it there as he talked and when he finished, he lowered it.

John jumped in his car and sped off like the devil was on his tail!

"I don't know what the officer said to him, but John has never set foot on my property since that day."

William slapped the table lightly. "Bully for our police! I would like to shake the hand of that Constable!"

She laughed. "You have! Many times. My knight in shining armor was Chief Inspector Rowan; although he was just a flatfoot then."

William, still a little in the dark, took it all in for a moment. There were pieces to this puzzle he was not seeing. All he could manage to say was, "I... I didn't know, Dana."

She shrugged. "Why would you? It's not something I share with the world. Not that I regretted my choice, except for the fact that I had no income for the house! So, when the bruises faded and I healed, I came to work for you." She smiled and wiped her eyes dry. "And now you know."

There were many more questions that William would have liked to ask, but he sensed she had spent enough emotion for one night.

"I think we should follow Charlie's advice for now."

She reached over and squeezed his hand. "Thank you." She stood up and collected their mugs. "How about I make some fresh drinks and we talk about something else."

He smiled broadly, "I would like that! This time, a little more Dirty in the Henie please!"

7

Collin and Catherine found William and Dana in the kitchen the next morning. Both were stifling yawns as they ate a hasty breakfast.

"What's with you two?" Catherine asked. "Did the new boss keep you up late?"

"It was the hot chocolate." Willian said cryptically, his eyes flickering to Dana. "Though our new Master of the house woke me at an ungodly hour. I never knew he got up so early."

"Thank God I was up at dawn to telephone in my grocery order for today's delivery," Dana said as she put eggs and toast on plates for the younger couple. "Or he might have pulled me out of bed too!"

"He pulled you out of bed?" Catherine asked William.

"By my feet."

Collin shook his head. "Where's the little emperor now?"

William sighed and rolled his eyes, "Well... after helping him dress, serving him breakfast, and listening to almost an hour of instructions, he is currently in the Conservatory sipping tea and reading my...his morning paper."

"What kind of instructions takes an hour?" Catherine asked.

"Oh, you shall soon hear. He made me memorize each word. Eat your breakfast. The master wishes to address us all before his guests arrive. Now, I better go see if he needs more tea."

He turned to go, then stopped and said to Collin, "There are clothes laid out for you in Ozaki's...err...my room. You're to change into them."

Collin's eyes popped open. He had taken great pains when he dressed this morning to look the part of a chauffeur. His jack boots were gleaming, his flared trousers neatly creased, and the high collared, button-down black jacket was spotless. A pair of black driving gloves and a cap rounded off the ensemble. He couldn't look any more the part!

"Why do I have to change?" Collin asked around a mouthful of eggs. "I look damn good in these rags!"

"Mr. Ozaki decided you would be of better use as a houseboy. Congratulations, you're being promoted."

Catherine giggled at the look on Collin's face. "I knew I married a go-getter!"

Collin found a pair of straight trousers, a white shirt, house-cut jacket and a pair of black oxfords. He sighed as he switched apparel. After he changed, he was on his way to the stairs when he saw William checking his attire in a full-length mirror in what was usually his room.

William had transformed himself into the stereotypical butler. He wore a dark black suit with a long-tailed jacket, starched white shirt, and black shoes that gleamed. A starched high collar, cummerbund, and spats rounded off the look sharply. He was adjusting his crisp bow tie when he noticed Collin. He stepped into the hallway and headed down the staircase.

"How come I don't have a tie?" Collin asked, falling in step. "Or do I have to wait for my next promotion?"

His Uncle gave him a withering look as they skipped down the stairs. "Get it out of your system now, Collin! The curtain is about to go up!" They reached the bottom of the stairs. "Now, take your place next to Catherine...and stand up straight. I hear him coming." He gave them all a stern look, "Remember your parts!"

Mr. Ozaki came out of the hallway that led to the Conservatory, swaggering like a conquering Mongol. He stepped up to face the line, but his sole attention was on William. The other three were no different from the furniture in the room.

"You may begin."

William gave a small bow then stepped out to face his co-workers. "These are the instructions of Mr. Ozaki. Catherine, you will ready the rooms for our esteemed guests. Make sure there are plenty of towels and amenities. Aside from Mr. Ozaki's brother, there will be a woman and an elderly gentleman. Adjust the accommodations where they are needed."

Catherine had no idea what he meant, but wisely just nodded.

"Collin" William went on. "You will assist Catherine in preparing the rooms until you're needed for your usual duties." He gave Collin a hard look. "You are under her supervision and will follow her orders explicably!"

When Collin just stared back at him in disbelief, William narrowed his eyes and Catherine nudged him in the ribs.

"Yes Sir". He stammered. "Explicably Sir!"

William went on, "Our guest will be arriving at the train station on the two p.m. train from New York. At one p.m., Collin, you will clean yourself up and change back into your chauffer outfit. You will be in the first spot of the waiting area, no later than one-thirty. You will escort our guests from the train to the car-with minimal conversation. Bring them directly here."

Collin took in a breath to reply, but William glared at him and turned to Dana. "Mrs. Woods, shortly after the guests arrive, they will have tea. Prepare some finger sandwiches and any accompaniments you have. Dinner shall be at seven, sharp. Tonight, our guest will dine on fish. Serve it with rice and whatever fresh vegetables you think are fit to eat this time of year. You will include a large basket of biscuits." His eyes flicked to Ozaki and back to her with a pleading look. "Please do not overcook the fish in the usual New England manner. Be sure it's light and delicate."

Dana's eyes had a glint in them as she deadpanned. "We don't have any fish, sir! I was going to roast some beef."

Ozaki wheeled on William, "No Beef! Fish." He pointed at the doors that led to the terrace. "There is a river below us. Surly a cook would have some sense in procuring some! If not, after he finishes the polishing, send the boy to catch some."

"I've never caught a fish in my life!" Collin protested.

Catherine turned to him, hands on hips and asked incredulously, "You've never been fishing? What did you do in the summer between boarding schools?"

He shrugged. "I grew up in the city. I--"

"Enough!" Ozaki growled. "Be still! I will have none of your whining!" He gestured to William to get back in the row, and then he put his hands on his hips and glared at the four of them. Slowly pacing before them, he said in a menacing tone,

"My family are descended from a long line of Samurai! Samurai expect obedience, not excuses, nor idle chatter. My brother is a great statesman and deserves great respect! You will speak only when spoken to and never in a familiar way! You will remember your place. You have your instructions - carry them out!"

He looked at William. "I will be in my room. Inform me the moment my guests arrive." That said, he stomped up the stairs and into his room, shutting the door behind him.

The other three turned and stared at William, who was smiling and rubbing his hands with glee. "I think we're going to pull this off!"

8

Catherine took Collin in tow and showed him where the cleaning supplies were kept and then to fetch clean linen for the rooms. She then led him up to the first guest bedroom. While she put fresh sheets on the bed and dusted, she delegated scrubbing the bathroom to Collin. He grumbled under his breath but after removing his jacket and donning a smock, then took the bucket with the rags and scrubbing powder from Catherine and went to it.

A few moments later, she heard fierce coughing from the bathroom and saw Collin, kneeling next to the bathtub in a cloud of dust. She rolled her eyes and went to see what the problem was. Hands on her hips, she asked crossly. "What is going on in here?"

Collin twisted around and held up the can of cleaner and the rag. "I'm doing what you told me! Scrubbing the tub like a scullion!" He poured some more dry powder on the rag and began to vigorously rub the inside of the porcelain. A fresh cloud of dust came up. "I don't think this stuff works very well!"

She quickly stepped over and took the cleaners out of his hand. "You idiot! You need to wet it! Make a paste then rub with it!" She ran the tub a moment and wet the rag. She put it in the pile of cleaner that had settled to the bottom of the tub and soon had it foamy. She stood and handed the rag back to Collin.

"How could someone who runs a theatrical empire not know that?"

"My empire has janitors who do these things!", he snarled back. He was not used to being called an idiot. "Where I come from, a bath is drawn. When I am finished, I step out, dry off, and never give it another thought."

She sighed and shook her head. "If you had three brothers, parents, and the occasional dog, believe me, you'd know how to scrub a tub!"

"Well, I never did, and I never intend to again! We have people to make sure our baths are fresh and clean! Our children will too!"

Catherine's eyes crossed and her cheeks bloomed red in anger. "Then you'll have another generation of lazy, helpless lay-abouts, Collin Frohman! I have no intention of raising a brood of spoiled, silver spoon sucking brats, with no work ethic or basic housekeeping skills! My children will make their own beds and do the occasional dishes and they'll be better people for it! And a good father would feel the same way!"

"Are you saying I wouldn't be a fit father?" he asked in a menacing tone.

Catherine was about to retort snidely, but after a moment's hesitation, her features went slack, and tears welled in her eyes. She sighed, "We have work to do."

Collin, concerned about her emotions, said "Alright, alright! No need for the water works. I'll play the scullion!" He pushed up his sleeves and attacked the tub with a vengeance.

Catherine nodded and turned to go back to her dusting. Before she left the bathroom, she said over her shoulder. "When you're done with that, I'll show you the art of toilet cleaning."

Collin froze in shock, and she added sweetly, "Call me first- I don't want you to drown!"

It was over an hour later when William came into the kitchen. Dana, none too happy about the change in her menu, opened her mouth to give him an earful. He staved off her venting by waving a piece of paper like a triumphant flag.

"Done! It took six telephone calls and a considerable slice out of this month's food budget, but Andy Long is bringing five large shad he caught this very morning! He should be here within the hour!"

"Fine.", Dana replied and put the last item in a crate. "Then you can make some room by taking this out to the tomb." The tomb was what Charles Frohman had dubbed the food storage room across the drive because it was dug into a hill and held all the 'dead' things.

William flinched, and then shrugged. "I shall be happy to!" He picked up the box and headed for the door when Dana stopped him. She fished a key ring off a peg next to the stove and dropped it into the box. "You'll need the key. Now, go on with you!"

He laughed and went out. It was not more than a few minutes until she realized she had just sent her boss on an errand. She was amazed at how this act seemed so natural.

When William returned, Dana offered him a cup of coffee.

"Ah! You are a gem! Thank you. Are you having a cup?" He smiled and winked at her, "Or do you only drink 'Dirty Heinis'?"

She laughed and sat next to him. "I wish I could, but I'm sure you would get tired of me running my mouth." She looked down and said, "You heard enough of my claptrap last night. Things I should have kept to myself."

William looked at her kindly then took a sip of his coffee.

"Claptrap? I don't' remember any claptrap! No, just some idle chatter among friends. I don't really recall any of the specifics!"

She smiled gratefully at him. "You are a sweet man, William." Before she thought about it, she leaned over and kissed him on the cheek. They looked at each other, startled, then set their mugs down and got to their feet. Dana smoothed the front of her skirt and headed to the stove. "Well, coffee break is over. I've got to get the sides ready for the shad."

"Yes, and I have to check on our custodians!" William announced, stealing one more gulp of coffee. "Will there be lunch?"

"I'll call you," she answered, then flapped a hand at him, "now, let me get back to work!"

He inclined his head and gave her a deep theatrical bow before he spun smartly on his heels and went into the pantry. He could still feel the kiss on his cheek and wondered how natural it felt.

9

The next hour passed quickly. William checked on the couple and their cleaning but left them alone when he found them working like bees. He noted a distinct chill in the air of the last bedroom they were finishing up but had too much to do to spend time trying to figure out the reason. Instead, he sent Collin to change just as Dana called them all down to lunch.

Catherine and William were at the counter when Collin came in wearing his uniform.

Catherine turned her head away in a petulant way, but Dana beamed at Collin. "My! You look quite dapper in the uniform."

"Thank you," he replied with a smile, and then he tugged on his belt buckle. "The pants are a little loose." He flicked his eyes in Catherine's direction. "Miss Legree worked me like a dog all morning! How about some lunch? I'm starving."

Dana laughed and handed him a plate. He glanced over at the empty chair next to where Catherine was sitting and proceeded to eat standing up, shoveling the food into his mouth.

Catherine rolled her eyes and looked disgusted. William held out a napkin to him. "Don't get anything on your shirt, Collin! And hurry! You must leave if you're to get to the station on time.

"Before you go, I'd like to address the cast. When Collin returns with our guests, the curtain will go up! Just act natural and let me run any interference. If we do our parts, we should have no problem pulling the wool over Ozaki's family's eyes." He looked pointedly at Collin, then Catherine. "Remember, we must work together. It's only a few days and it will pass quickly."

"And Christmas with it!" Collin grumbled.

William heaved a great sigh, but it was Dana who stepped in. "Collin, Christmas isn't all eggnog and mistletoe. It's about family, friends, and love. What we're about to do has everything with that!"

"Well said!" William chimed in.

Collin nodded and smiled, then looked at William sideways. "Well, you did promise me a Christmas we wouldn't forget!"

"That's the spirit, Collin!" William clapped him on the shoulder.

Collin looked over to Catherine, who has lost her anger in the moment. He stepped over and kissed her on the cheek.

"Break a leg, darling!" Then he left to get his car.

As soon as he left the room, William turned to Catherine. "Is there going to be a problem with you two? I don't wish to pry into your affairs, but we all need to work together."

"We'll be fine." she assured him. "I just never knew what a spoiled rich brat he was until I put him to work. Honestly! He's just so ignorant of the basic chores in life! Sometimes, I think he has more money than sense!"

Dana tilted her head and crossed her arms over her chest. "I doubt you minded his money when you were painting the town red in New York!"

Catherine recoiled like she was slapped, and Dana went to her and put an arm around her shoulder to take the sting out of her words. "Look, Collin was raised differently than us. We are used to our roles and William is the greatest actor in America! Collin will need a little more patience, but his heart is in the right place."

"You needn't worry about Collin." William declared. "He may grumble and carp, but he's got backbone! He'll come through in the end, just like his father. Now, I'll tidy up here while you two go to freshen up and change into a clean uniform! Our lord and master wishes to inspect us before his family arrives."

Dana's eyebrows raised. "Getting freshened up for Osaki's inspection is an offer we won't refuse! Come along Catherine." Dana stopped abreast of William and batted her eyes at him. "Should we shave our legs for the inspection?"

William blushed and the two women scurried out in peals of giggles.

The three of them were lined up near the foyer, looking crisp and clean when the door to William's room opened. The man who paused at the top of the stairs hardly resembled Ozaki at all. He had the same height and build, but there was nothing familiar about his persona. He looked down at them, like Genghis Khan would from atop a mountain of skulls.

He was wrapped from head to shins in an oriental silken robe of sea green with bright white trim at the billowing cuffs, hem, and lapels, and fastened around his waist by a dark green sash. He wore an expensive suit beneath the robe, with a crisp bow tie beneath his chin and polished leather shoes peeked from beneath creased dark trousers. As he started down the stairs, William noticed the glint of the cuff links. They were enormous diamonds in a platinum setting. Collin's father had given them to William after the first successful run of Sherlock Holmes, which had made them both a lot of money. He was not sure if he liked seeing them on Ozaki, but he had to admit they were the perfect touch to his new image. He looked like a man who had made his wealth in America, but still honored his native country. Besides, he did tell Ozaki that whatever was in the castle was his for the next few days.

He looked physically different also because he had greased his hair so it swept from front to back. He looked ten years younger.

He slowly made his way down the stairs at a stately pace. Hands behind his back, he said nothing as he stood before them, half lidded eyes looking them up and down.

The three of them stared back, as if seeing him for the first time, until Catherine said, in semi-awe "You look wonderful, Mr. Ozaki."

Ozaki's face softened and he might have broken character with a kind response, but a car horn sounded from outside. The arrogance snapped right back.

"They have arrived, William! What are you waiting for? Greet them at the door and bring them to me." He turned and glared at the girls. "Make yourselves presentable at the top of the steps to greet my guests!" With that, he walked a few paces away and turned to wait, not once even glancing at the girls.

William made it down to the steps just in time as the door opened and Collin came in. He rolled his eyes then went to the kitchen and up the back staircase to change into a houseboy coat. He made the switch then went to join the ladies standing in a line at attention.

William swung the door open and a well-dressed, stately Japanese man stood in the threshold, flanked by an older man and a woman.

"Good afternoon, gentlemen." He inclined his head and addressed the woman. "Madame."

The younger man puffed up his chest. "I am Yukio Ozaki, and I am here to see my brother." He gave William a slight incline of his head. His manner was a bit pompous, but his eyes were as big as saucers as he looked about the gigantic space behind William.

William smiled slightly. "Of course. You are expected. Welcome to the Seven Sisters." He bowed deeply then backed up to give them room to enter.

William led them up the steps into the great room. As they passed the staff, the women curtsied, and Collin bowed deeply as they were instructed to. The three Asians never gave them a glance.

Yukio and Ozaki stared at each other for a moment, emotions playing across Ozaki's face as he saw his brother for the first time in nearly twenty-five years. Yukio broke into a wide grin and rushed forward to throw his arms around his brother.

"Yukitaka! It is good to see you!" he stepped back but kept his hands on Ozaki's shoulders. "It has been too long!"

Ozaki seemed to relax and smiled back at his brother. "It has, brother." He tore his eyes off his brother and bowed to the other two with him.

"Welcome to my humble home."

Yukio straightened up and said, "May I introduce my esteemed Uncle, Samata Torido." The old man bowed. "And his daughter, Miko". The woman bowed deeply.

The woman said something in her native tongue and the conversation continued in Japanese. William took the opportunity to gesture for the servants to step over and take their coats.

Dana stepped right over and curtsied to Yukio, holding out her arms to take his coat. Yukio shrugged out of his coat and handed it to her with a smile, along with his hat and cane. Dana bowed slightly and took a few steps backwards before turning and going back to her spot.

Collin, 'Tres Gallant' in his mind, went to help the woman off with her coat and tossed it over his arms. Ozaki and his brother were back in deep conversation and so they did not notice when the woman's face scrunched up and she hissed as she pulled off her gloves quickly, revealing long blood red colored nails. She leaned in close and clamped a hand on his forearm. Collin was sure the nails went right through his coat and shirt and with the slightest bit more pressure would have drawn blood.

She snarled, "Hang that coat carefully, boy! If there is one wrinkle on it, I will have you beaten!"

The rage left her face and was replaced by a crocodile smile as she turned back to the men. Shocked, Collin followed Dana's lead, but more because he did not want to turn his back on the dragon lady.

Catherine was smiling and talking softly to the old man as she gently helped him remove his coat and hat. He gave her a toothless smile and reached up to gently pat her face. Catherine smiled and blushed slightly, but the look dropped from her face when she turned away and it was replaced by one of mild outrage. The blush on her cheeks deepened.

She stomped over to the other two, eyes wide, and whispered, "That old man patted my rear end."

When a chuckle burst out of Collin, she glared at him.

He kept his expression neutral, and dead panned. "You want me to bust him in the chops? I'm not afraid of him." He rubbed his forearm where the woman had gripped him. "Just as long as I don't have to tangle with the dragon lady!"

They began to bicker in whispers when William came over to them, his eyes bulging over a stern expression. "What is going on here?"

Catherine wheeled on him, "When I took his coat like you instructed, that disgusting old man put his hand on my bottom!"

"I'm sure it was an accident." William said soothingly. "A man of his age has less control of his movements."

She glared at him and said through clenched teeth. "He squeezed it!"

Collin added to the attack. "And that hag of a woman wasn't in this house five minutes, and she threatened to have me beaten! If that's how his family is, I say we tell them the truth and put them back on the train!"

William held up his hands. "Please, everyone, settle down. The woman and the old man, in fact, are not Ozaki's family. At least, not by blood. The woman is Yukio's sister-in-law, and the old man is her uncle. I didn't catch their names, the introductions were in Japanese, and extremely fast Japanese at that! Their names don't matter to us anyways – as far as we are concerned, they are Madam and Sir." He rubbed his hands in glee. "Since they have never met Ozaki, they will be easier to hoodwink! Imagine the stories they'll tell when they get home! Ozaki will be legend in his hometown! You two," he pointed at Collin and Catherine, "just need to stay out of their reach."

They both started to protest, but William overrode them. "Please! I'll keep a close eye on things. We must stick to the script!

"Now, you two get their luggage and take it up to their rooms. Yukio will go in the second bedroom, the sister-in-law and uncle in the second and third. Collin, take your cues from Catherine. She knows what to do." He dismissed them and turned to Dana. She waited until the couple was heading down the stairs to the foyer to fetch the bags before she said to William in a low menacing voice, "I can't believe you'd let them be treated that way!"

William sighed and took her by the arm into the hallways, out of sight of the guests. "You must understand, the customs of the Japanese are much more rigid between the classes. It's just the way their society works."

She gave him a level look in return and said, "Then its best I stay in the kitchen. and if any of them lays hands on me, I'll give them a taste of an American custom! My cast iron fry pan upside their head!"

William noted the stern look on Dana's face and replied. "Duly noted. Very well, Mr. Ozaki would like tea and something to snack on. I'll serve it when it's ready."

She smiled and answered. "Twenty minutes," before she started walking away. She stopped suddenly as something occurred to her. "William, while you were puttering around in my kitchen, did you move my oven mitts? The thick brown ones with the tassels?"

He had no idea what she was talking about and told her so.

She frowned. "Funny...I have no idea where they went."

10

After the guests had freshened up, William gathered them and led them to the sitting area in the great room, where Ozaki awaited them. After they settled into seats, Ozaki flicked a hand at William, and he dashed off to get the refreshments. When he returned, he found everyone smiling and relaxed.

He served the tea, with all the aplomb of a headwaiter in a great restaurant, and carefully watched to see how things were working out. He had no idea of their family dynamics, as they were speaking Japanese, so he had to rely on his knowledge of body language.

Ozaki and his brother were doing most of the talking and their speech was punctuated by bursts of laughter, so, William reasoned that their reunion was like many other brothers. Time and distance meant little to blood and William was pleased to see Ozaki looking confident and at ease. If he couldn't see any signs that Ozaki was out of place, he doubted his long absent brother would.

The old man just stared straight ahead, seemingly oblivious to his surroundings, with his hands resting on the upright cane between his legs. Once and a while, he would thump the cane on the floor and bark out a word or short phrase. They would smile politely at him and return to their conversation.

The dragon lady did make him a bit nervous. The crocodile smile was glued to her face, and her eyes were sharp and searching as she sized up the castle and William himself. He had the feeling she was the kind of woman who could tell you exactly what your socks cost. They would need to take special care around her.

All in all, things were going splendid so far.

William, for his part, was light on his feet and silent in his movements, as he served with the perfect balance of attentiveness and respectful distance from the master and his guests. He reveled in his role, immensely pleased to see Ozaki's family looking at his friend and the castle with admiration. He was beyond acting and had become the perfect butler. He was confident in his abilities and found their ignorance of his true self more satisfying that all the applause and calls for 'Encore' he had experienced in his long career. This role would be his opus magnum, unscripted and in the moment. Even though only a very few would know of his performance, He would know.

Perhaps what helped fuel his high spirits, was all the interaction he suddenly had with Dana. Working with her instead of her working for him had opened up another side to her personality that William found enchanting. She was quite intelligent and quick to laugh as she dropped a layer of formality that she always showed her employer. William found himself letting down his walls before her and when their eyes met, he felt a sensation that he had not felt for years. He knew that it might only last as long as their charade, but William hoped some of the newfound closeness would last after things went back to normal. Of course, she might not see things in the same light and it would not do to let their situation become awkward. It was a quandary that all his years of playing the great detective could not solve.

When William thought that Ozaki and his guests had all they needed for the moment, he slipped away to the kitchen to see how the others were doing. Catherine and Collin had finished stowing the luggage and he had put them to polishing the dinnerware for later.

He came into the pantry area as they stood facing a sideboard polishing silverware. Collin finished a fork and set it in the stack between them. William was about to greet the two but remained still when she picked up the fork Collin had set down and eyed it. She sighed and began to polish it anew.

"What?" Collin asked. "Now I can't polish a fork right?"

William could sense her shoulders tense, but she replied in a calm tone. "You left some polish between the tines, Collin. Do you want to make somebody sick?"

Collin snorted. "Ozaki is going to need some polish if he's going to fool that brother of his!"

Catherine threw her cloth on the table and put her hands on her hips. "What has gotten into you? You've been carping about Ozaki all morning! If anyone should be complaining, it should be William! He's the one who had to turn everything over to his valet!"

"Everything but his identity!"

"I don't think my father would have appreciated Ozaki pretending to have his life, not to mention taking credit for all his accomplishments! It's an insult to his memory! Why couldn't he pretend to be, oh I don't know…a banker. Or better yet, a railroad tycoon! Jessum crow! There's a railway right outside the door for God's sake!"

Catherine rolled her eyes and sighed. William thought this a good moment to intervene.

"When the two of you are through with the silverware, I want you to go over the second floor again. Everything must be pristine for our guests. Catherine-you know what to do." He gave Collin a stern look. "Stay in character and, please, watch what you say out loud! You know how sound carries in this house!"

He walked away before Collin could make a smart remark. Dana was bustling about in the warm kitchen and William walked right past her to flop into a chair by the window counter.

She saw the look on his face and stopped what she was doing.

"What is it William? You're upset." Her eyes narrowed, "Has Ozaki been at you again?"

"No, no. Nothing like that. The king is holding court very well, in fact. It's Collin that has me worried. Apparently, he is not too happy with Ozaki pretending to be his father, Charlie, though; I do not know what he expected. Ozaki was honest with him from the start. It's not like Ozaki could pull off being an American actor! And Catherine tells me that he has not been to church in months. That he has abandoned God in his anger over his father's death. This simply won't do!"

William went up another notch in her eyes and it warmed her. Not many friends would worry about another's soul!

"Don't worry so, William. Collin will keep his word. He won't spoil the plan." She smiled at him,

"Besides, this is the season for miracles. The more he tries to push away, the tighter God will hold him! Now, let me fix you a cup of coffee. You look like you need one."

William started to shake his head, and then went still. His eyes widened and a sly smile came across his face. He looked down at Dana and winked.

"Perhaps I can nudge him in the right direction. I must take a raincheck on that coffee, dear lady. I need to make a telephone call from the study." The smile dropped off his face. "What's more, perhaps worse, is that I am afraid our little act is taking a toll on Collin and Catherine's relationship. Working together seems to rub them the wrong way."

Dana nodded sagely. "Maybe they need a break from each other. On your way out, send Collin in to see me. I need some help. Then I'll give him back to Catherine."

"Oh, yes, I see the fish has been delivered."

Dana was mildly surprised. "How did you know that? I put it in the icebox an hour ago and it's far too fresh to smell!"

William chuckled and pointed behind her. She turned to see three cats sitting at the base of the icebox, looking at it as if it was a play in itself, while two paced across the top, sniffing and pawing at the seal on the icebox.

She turned back to William, who bowed deeply with a flourish.

"I shall send your knight in to save the damsel in distress!"

She snorted. "I don't need a savior-I need a scaler!"

William was just finishing his call when he heard the bell ringing from the great room. The master needed of him!

Ozaki picked up the bell for the second time and rang it with vigor. Moments later, William walked quickly up to the group and bowed slightly to Ozaki. Ozaki glared up at him, his eyes flickering to the bell on the table.

"Pardon my delay, Sir. I was...instructing the cook."

The dragon lady nodded sharply and spoke. "Every good cook needs a beating now and then!"

Ozaki and his brother smiled, but the old man thumped his cane on the ground in agreement.

"Perhaps I shall take your advice" Ozaki replied pleasantly. "She is long overdue!" Then he turned to William. "My guests would like a tour of my home. We will begin now."

William knew Ozaki well enough to know what he meant. He expected William to guide the tour because if he did it himself, it would look like he was being immodest. That, and no one knew the castle better than William.

"If it pleases you, sir. We can start on the top floor and work our way down." William was sure that Collin would be out of sight by the time they reached the main floor.

Ozaki rose to his feet and flicked a hand at William. "Get on with it then!" He turned to his family and bowed. "If you would care to follow me?"

Since they had already seen the second floor, that was mostly bedrooms and utility closets, Willian was leading the troop up the stairs to the third floor, where the art gallery was. Pausing at the railing that overlooked the great room, Yukio gazed about his surroundings in wonder. He turned to Ozaki,

"How did you manage all this, brother? It is... quite impressive!"

Ozaki, having been with William from long before the start of the construction, knew more than enough to bluff his way through the narrative. William stood stoically to the side as Ozaki described how he designed the steel frame, procured the native stone that made the walls of the castle, built the tramway from the river to bring the materials up, and he finished by describing the unique looks and handles to the large oak doors and windows that he had 'talked' an Amish craftsman through. By the time he was done, his guests were in awe and William wanted to toss him over the railing. Only years of honing his craft on the stage kept Ozaki from taking the plunge. He would never break character.

The tour resumed and the stairs were a challenge, as they had to make their way at a snail's pace, so the old man could keep up. Even with some assistance from Miko and Ozaki's brother, William was starting to wonder if they would get there by nightfall.

As soon as they entered to open gallery area, they quickly set the old man on a viewing bench, and he was nodding off almost immediately. William and Ozaki exchanged looks worrying that the old man might fall over, but Yukio and the dragon lady seemed unconcerned. William stepped to the side, within reach of the old man and Ozaki strolled through the room with his brother and the dragon lady.

The only two changes made to the gallery was to add two of Ozaki's paper screens, set in a way that bisected the rooms and kept them walking in one direction. There was not much conversation, but William was not worried about any questions that might be asked. Ozaki knew as much about the pieces as he did, having been there almost every time he acquired one. His calves began to ache from standing in one spot as they finally made their circuit of the rooms.

Ozaki's brother stood and admired a particular piece. William was hoping to hear a comment on it, preferably in English. Instead, the dragon lady spoke,

"Ozaki-Sama," She purred. "Forgive me for asking in my ignorance, but you have no Japanese artists in your gallery. Do you prefer Western art to our own?"

Ozaki smiled slyly. "Sun Tze said, 'Know your enemy before you take the field' Gai-Jin art gives me insight into the western mind that has helped me dominate them."

Ozaki's brother glared at her. Her question bordered on rudeness. "I find the art of all cultures to be beautiful, each in their own way."

Ozaki smiled and nodded at him. He turned to the dragon lady. "Of course, I would wish to have more of our fine artist's work. I have a few small pieces in my study I would be honored to show you.

Unfortunately, little of our artwork leaves Japan and it is difficult to find."

"Nonsense!" Ozaki's brother replied. "I will send you a few pieces when I return home! And you have no need to apologize, Brother! This painting in front of me is magnificent! The artist captures the raw power of the sea with the imagery of a simple fisherman. I've seen many of our artists try to replicate this scene, but none do it with such masterful brush strokes!"

Ozaki beamed at the compliment. "You like it? It's yours!"

"Oh No, Yukitaka! I could not accept!"

Ozaki held up a hand to forestall any more protests. "Nonsense! It is nothing!" He turned to William. "Have this crated and ready to travel with my brother. And be careful! I want it looking as good on his wall as it does on mine!"

William froze in shock, unable to speak, but managing to nod.

It was his Winslow Homer masterpiece.

11

William carried the Winslow down the stairs looking like he bore a casket. He set it down in the great room, his mind furiously trying to think of a way to keep it, but he could not embarrass his man by turning him into an Indian giver. His mind turned to ways of making Ozaki pay when Osaki's family went home.

He quickly sped them through the library and study – there were too many things that might trip them up, but he took his time in the great room. The player piano fascinated them, and he was forced to play three paper rolls of tunes before they moved on. The sun was beginning to set, and William wanted to finish the tour before dark. The tour ended in the conservatory, where William was to serve cocktails.

There was a brief commotion when Mike, or perhaps it was Lena, hopped out of the pool and began to croak for food. The dragon lady shrieked and scurried across the room, but the old man went on the offensive.

Quicker than his age belied, he jumped forward and tried to clobber the frog with his cane. Luckily, his eyesight was poor, and he only landed blows on the rock ledge on both sides of the pet before Ozaki's brother grabbed the cane and talked him into calming down. The frog gave him a smirk and jumped back into the safety of the pool.

William glared at Ozaki, who just looked back at him and said,

"I will have a Presbyterian, William. In fact, make us all one." He turned and spoke Japanese to his guests. Apologizing to the woman and explaining the pet frog. They crowed with delight when Ozaki took a few dead flies out of a sugar bowl and placed them into the pool. The large frog snapped them up with a long tongue as fast as lightning.

William returned with the drinks on a tray, and he included the bottle of Rye, a seltzer, and Ginger ale. When they were all set with their drinks, Ozaki dismissed William to see to dinner. William, still furious about his painting was in a tizzy when he stomped into the kitchen and threw himself into a chair by the window table.

After letting him huff for a few minutes, Dana calmly looked up from the winter shad she was checking for bones and asked, with a wry smile, "Tough matinee?"

Indignant, William sat up straight and declared, "Never have I treated any employee of mine so cavalier as Osaki is treating us...and I have never given away their possessions!"

"Now, William," Dana said in a soothing voice. "You told me yourself that the Japanese have strict attitudes, remember? If I can hold my tongue...well... You're an actor for Pete's sake!" Then she tilted her head. "Just what of yours did the little tyrant give away?"

"We were in the gallery and his brother was admiring one of my..." He began to sputter in anger. Dana's eyes flew open. "Oh, No! Not the Winslow?"

William could only nod. She put the pliers down and walked over to place her hands on his wrist and the other on his shoulder. Giving him a gentle shake. "I'm so sorry William. Whatever possess him to give your Winlow Homer painting to his brother?"

Before William could calm down enough to answer, Collin stalked into the room, holding both his reddened hands up. "Look what Catherine has done to me!" Catherine came into the room after him, carrying some cleaning rags. Collin pointed at her and claimed, "That woman is straight out of a Dicken's novel!" He stuck his hands out at William and Dana, with an overly dramatic look on his face. They were raw looking with prunes for fingertips.

"Look at these hands! I shall never play the violin again! Toilets, sinks, and tubs! Toilets, sinks, and tubs! Asides from the floors, walls, and windows!" He glared at William. "Did you even think about how hard it is to clean stone when you built this place?"

A rag hit him in the face and cut of his tirade. Everyone's gaze turned to Catherine, who was standing, fists on hips and beet red in the face.

"Stop whining, you big baby! If you can't stand a little cleaning, then how are you..." she clamped her mouth shut in mid-sentence and tears welled in her eyes.

Collin's confused expression was slowly turning to anger when Dana stepped in to smooth the waters. She stepped between the couple, her back to Collin and gently took the rags out of her hands. "Catherine, dear. Could you go out to the root cellar and find us some nice beets to go with the shad tonight? I believe they are in the back, left corner."

Catherine glared over her shoulder at her husband for another moment. She looked as if she had more to say, but Dana cut her off.

"Take a few deep breaths when you're outside." She looked her friend straight in the eye.

"Flat stones skip, round stones sink."

Catherine looked back at her for a moment and her facial features smoothed out. She nodded and headed for the door. Dana turned to Collin and waited for Catherine to get out of hearing range before she said softly, "Collin, you need to understand--"

"What I understand is that I need a drink!" He growled and turned on his heels to go out the way he came in. Dana sighed at his back and turned to see William staring at her, a stunned look on his face.

"What was that all about? And what was all that about skipping stones? It sounded like something Ozaki would say!"

Dana stepped up to him. "Confucius couldn't hold a candle to Granny! Hot words are like throwing a flat stone into a pond. It will just skip along, making ripples on the water everywhere it touches. Ripples that keep spreading, causing more strife.

Calm words are like a round stone: when you toss that in, it makes a big splash, and it quickly sinks in."

Before William could comment, Collin stormed back into the kitchen, a tall glass of clear liquid in his hands. The sharp tang of juniper berries overrode the smell of the dinner filets.

Dana cast an eye on him then went to the sideboard where she picked up a bowl of potatoes and a peeler. She placed them in front of a sulking Collin and ordered, "You can sulk and swill, young man, but you'll do it peeling those potatoes! And be quick about it! I want to get them on the stove shortly."

Collin rolled his eyes and ran a hand over his head. "Look, Dana, she's been running roughshod on me all day…"

"And your day's not over!" Dana cut him off. "Now, start peeling!"

Collin looked as if he was going to refuse but wilted under Dana's calm stare. He took a swig of his drink and began to attack the potatoes like they had done him wrong.

Catherine came in with the beets and set them next to the bowl. She glared at the drink, then at her husband. "I suppose a well-bred gentleman always has a Martini when he does scullion work?"

The peeler froze in mid slash and Collin replied in a low menacing tone. "At least it's the spuds being peeled." He raised his eyes at his wife. "And not me!"

The kitchen went silent. Catherine looked as if she was going to explode, but then she regained her composure and replied calmly, "We can talk about this later."

Collin dropped his eyes and went back to his chore. "Damn straight we will!"

Suddenly, Ozaki burst into the scene. The little man stumbled slightly as he crossed the threshold, barely keeping from going down next to Collin's chair. He quickly righted himself and put his hands behind his back to steady himself. When William saw the glazed look on Ozaki's face, he slowly rose off his seat.

Ozaki swayed slightly for a minute, his eyes were glassy and unfocused. He opened his mouth to speak, but no sound came out. Collin's eyebrows shot up and a grin slowly split his face as he realized what he was seeing.

"What are you doing?" he blurted out.

Ozaki snapped back into focus and snarled at him. "Keep your hands moving and your mouth shut, houseboy!" He seized the lapels of his jacket with both hands and announced, slurring slightly, "I have come to consult with the cook about dinner!"

William saw the look of surprise on Dana's face, and he noted the annoyance. Dana was the queen of her kingdom and, charade or not, no one 'consulted' her. They ate what she made.

Thankfully, William did not have to step in. Ozaki saw the fillets of Shad on the table and zeroed in on them. He stepped over and leaned over to inspect the long slabs of pale meat. He made a great show of sniffing them and running a finger over the surface. The matching sacs of roe wrapped in bacon gave him pause, but he simply mumbled something in Japanese and shrugged. He straightened up and gave Dana a condescending nod.

"Excellent! Be sure to cook it lightly. I want moist flakes, not shoe leather! And be sure to fry the roe. The bacon crispy, yet the eggs barely warmed!"

Dana's eyes crossed and she held the boning pliers in a white-knuckle grip. William decided that now was a good time to step in.

"If I may ask, Sir, where are the guests?"

Ozaki puffed up his chest and barked. "I showed them to their rooms so they could rest and freshen up before dinner. Someone had to while you were lollygagging around! Now, I am going to do the same!" His eyes narrowed and he commanded, "Dinner at seven-thirty sharp!"

With that, he turned on his heels to leave but spun too far and ended up facing Catherine. "Ah! There you are! You are doing an excellent job, Catherine. Remind me to give you a raise!"

Then he turned to Collin and reached over to pluck his glass off the table. Sticking his face close to Collin, he snarled. "No drinking on the job! Keep your hands off my liquor!" With that, he strode out of the room, bumping into the doorframe.

Catherine said, in a puzzled tone, "What was that all about?"

"That's pretty obvious!" Dana said with a giggle. "Our Mr. Ozaki has been dipping his bill!"

William shook his head. "I hope he wakes up in time for dinner! I guess I should never have left the bottle with him. Ozaki rarely imbibes and doesn't hold his liquor very well."

"Well, the little rat had no trouble holding mine!" Collin groused as he got to his feet. "That's it! I'm done with this farce! The little tyrant can fall flat on his face for all I care. I'm taking Catherine and we're heading back to the city- where we can still have a normal Christmas."

"We are not going anywhere!" Catherine fumed. "If you want to go back to Yonkers and have Christmas by yourself-Go ahead! I'm staying here with my family and friends. We made a promise and someone in this family is going to keep their word!"

Collin slapped the peeler on the table and drew a great breath and looked as if he would breathe fire. William quickly stepped forward and took him by the shoulders before he could erupt.

"Now Collin, you don't really mean that. You love Ozaki as much as we all do. Look, it's been a long day for all of us. Why don't you and Catherine take the rest of the night off? Go back to the Polly and relax. Dana and I can handle dinner.

"Tomorrow is Christmas Eve, I'm sure everyone will be in better spirits."

Catherine turned to Dana. "Oh, no! I couldn't leave all that work to the two of you."

"Nonsense." Dana replied. "Just help with the set up and we can take it from there. William, you take Catherine and set the table and Collin and I will finish getting dinner ready."

Catherine reluctantly agreed and, even more so did Collin. Catherine looked at her husband and huffed, then followed William out to the dining room.

Dana pointed her pliers at Collin. "Finish peeling those potatoes, bucko."

When she was sure Collin was working, she started searching the tabletops and then the floor.

"Lose something?"

She straightened up with a puzzled look on her face.

"Have you seen the cozy I had on this table? I could swear I put it out to put the biscuits on!"

"What's a cozy?" Collin asked.

Catherine gave him a withering look as she picked up a stack of napkins and headed for the door. "It would look like a big coaster to you!"

12

The rest of the preparations went smoothly, if not a bit chilly between the young couple. William and Dana managed to keep them busy and apart so there were no more eruptions. Soon everything was set, and William walked the couple down to the foyer. Catherine donned her coat, scarf, and mittens while Collin fumbled about for his outerwear. Catherine stopped before the door and turned to William. "Are you sure about this?" She cast a stink eye on Collin, "I'm willing to stay and help. I'm not scared of a little honest work!"

Collin rolled his eyes and William stepped in, "I know that Catherine, but you've done more than enough already today." He glanced at Collin. "You both have! Dana and I can take it from here. We'll see you both in the morning."

With that, he opened the door, letting a rush of cold air swirl into the room and gave her a doorman's bow. She said goodnight and walked out into the frigid night.

Collin followed behind her, pulling the lapels of his jacket up as high as they would go.

"Night, Uncle Will." He shivered in the cold wind.

"Where's your hat?" William asked.

Collin shrugged and shook his head, "I have no idea. I could have sworn I hung it up right next to my coat, but I can't find it anywhere." He sighed and rushed out after his wife.

William trudged down the hallway to the kitchen, a dour look on his face. The plan was working but it was having a dire effect on two people he considered family. Not to mention how it would possibly ruin their first Christmas together. Collin is tossing aside his faith and Catherine's obvious disappointment in her husband's values tore at his heart, yet he had a plan to deal with one of the problems. Perhaps Dana would have some suggestions for the other.

Dana was just pulling out a pan of her famous biscuits when William entered the kitchen.

Setting the pan of shad down on the counter, she poked at one with a paring knife. Satisfied they were perfect, she turned and asked, "Do you think they'll be alright on the boat tonight? It's awfully cold on the river."

William snorted. "If I know those two, it will be even chillier INSIDE the Polly."

"Oh, I don't know about that," Dana replied lightly. "Young couples have their spats, and then they make up!" She winked at William, "That's why we start the fights in the first place!"

William laughed and feigned shock. "Why, Mrs. Woods! I'm knocked for six!"

They both laughed, but an incessant bell ringing filled the kitchen air. Ozaki was using the very silent alarm that William had put in to summon his valet at dinner. The button was set into the floor, so the other guests had no idea how the servants appeared when needed.

William sighed. "I hope you're right, Dana, but I'm worried."

The bell rang again, longer in duration this time.

"I'm assuming the guests have gathered at the table. Is everything ready?"

Dana nodded, "The fish is going in now. It will take a while, so go and do your little show. By the time they've had their salad, everything will be ready."

"Excellent!" He donned his black jacket and draped a white cloth over his left forearm. Letting his facial features go slack, he stood straight and put his nose in the air.

"Act Three. Scene one." Then he walked out of the kitchen at a stately pace.

Catherine and Collin pulled up to the Aunt Polly in silence, though it was obvious they both had a lot to say. The frigid wind off the river kept the scarf over Catherine's mouth and Collin was doing his best to cover his bare ears, so conversation was out. They were both happy when they crossed the dock and boarded the houseboat.

Catherine went in the salon doors, where it was out of the wind at least, while Collin hustled up the gangway to reach the pilothouse, as Catherine went right to their room, saying she was going to shower. He fired up the Aunt Polly's engines to put some heat running through the ducts, then stepped through the hatch to the kitchen, and headed for the salons' liquor cabinet.

As he passed the suite Catherine and he were using, Collin called out through the door, "The water should be hot soon. I'll be in the salon after you take your shower."

"What about dinner?" came a muffled reply.

"Make whatever you want. I'm hungry enough to eat anything!"

He thought he heard a bang but ignored it as he headed for a much-needed drink. After a while, Catherine came into the salon in her robe with a towel wrapped around her head. Collin, well into his second drink looked over at her and said, "And I suppose you think I drink too much!"

Catherine's eyes crossed, but she composed herself and brought a glass with chipped ice from behind her back. "Actually, I was thinking I don't drink enough!" She held her glass out to him.

"That's my girl!" Collin grinned and poured her a stiff whiskey, then added a touch of seltzer. Handing it to her, he asked, "What's for supper?"

Catherine took a long drought of her drink and answered. "I'm heating up some soup I found and there is bread and ham in the icebox."

Collin snorted softly, "Soup and sandwiches? Doesn't seem like much of a Christmas Eve... eve dinner."

"Oh, and what kind of dinner would that be?"

"Well, if we were in the city, we'd be at Rossi's, having a nice thick filet Mignon, or some Coquille ST. Jacques. Afterwards, we could have stopped by John and Mindy's bash for a nightcap with our friends."

Catherine sighed. "Your friends. They'll be having parties and drinking themselves silly long after the holidays are over. Aren't you the least bit happy to be here, with people who are family for the holidays? I know it isn't how you wanted to spend this season, but can't you at least be happy we're helping someone we love. With people who love us?"

Collin had a cutting quip on the tip of his tongue but bit it back when he saw the sadness in her eyes. He sighed.

"Of course, I want to help Ozaki! Truth be told, I am tickled to pull one over on that crowd. The brother seems alright, but that dragon lady and the old man! They give me the heebie-jeebies!"

Catherine said nothing and Collin drank the rest of his drink. With his eyes on the empty glass, he added. "And I didn't sign up to clean tubs and toilets all day and get scolded more than I did in school!"

Catherine pursed her lips. "I'm sorry I ran roughshod on you, honey, but...it's like you never lived in the real world. What would happen if you had to fend for yourself?" She looked him straight in the eye. "What if this was our life. No money, no mansions, no fancy cars? If I were still a maid and you were a houseboy? What would you teach our children?"

That rankled him. "Hey! I may not know the right way to scrub a tub, but I'm no idiot either! I run a huge company, remember? I may not have had to wash my own clothes or wash the dishes, but I didn't turn out too bad!"

She laughed, "Says the man who spent his education in the dean's office."

"Bah!" he flapped a hand at her, "Besides, dad left the family enough to live well the rest of our lives and, by the time I'm finished, they'll be enough for our children and their children besides! They will never want for anything!"

Catherine slowly put her empty glass on the table and Collin was shocked to see moisture in her eyes when she replied, "But they'll never earn anything." She stood. "I'll go check on the soup."

Collin watched her walk away, feeling he somehow failed in some way.

Dinner was finally over.

Dana hadn't seen much of William once dinner began. It seemed like he barely had time to come to the kitchen and reload the serving cart before the bell was ringing again. William looked almost ragged as he eased himself onto a stool at the counter. Dana set their nightcaps down in front of him. He breathed the minty sweet steam from the mug and gave her a grateful smile.

"I don't know why you have kept this elixir hidden from me all these years."

She laughed and countered, "You never looked like you needed it before the last few days. How did it go? I thought Ozaki was tap dancing on the bell button for a while!"

He took a sip of the drink. "Ozaki has certainly solidified into his role! His worship had me hopping all night long! Then, capping off his gifting away my Winslow, he had me open my finest bottles of wine. Which they swilled like a bunch of Bowery bums! During my life in the theater, I have seen quite a lot of drinking, but these people could hold their own with any of them!"

Dana saw the maudlin cast to his face, so she tried to change the subject "Your theater people seem quite interesting. I think I would like to meet some of them one day."

William smiled. "Well, I have no plans for the immediate future, but I'm certain to return to the stage at some point. I'll take you along if you wish."

She arched her eyebrows. "Now, that would be fun! I've never been backstage before!"

"Then you're in for a new experience! But I must warn you, watching a play from the wings will cast a whole new light on the production!" he winked at her. "And you must be discreet about what you witness. Half of the stage's allure is our illusions."

She shrugged. "Oh, I can keep my tongue behind my teeth, Lad." She smiled slyly, a twinkle in her eye. "I'm used to being hounded by half the town about you! They have the most predictable questions. What is he really like? What does he eat? Is he as smart as Sherlock Holmes?" She laughed, "Does he have a hundred cats?"

William laughed with her. "So, what did you tell them?"

She grew serious. "I told them you were a good and kind man, and a private one. You ate what I fed you, and that Mr. Sherlock Holmes couldn't hold a candle to your intelligence. Then I tell them to mind their own business!"

He laughed. "Funny, I never thought folks thought much about me since I stepped off the boards. An actor is only as good as his last review." He grew a bit somber. "I've been an actor so long I assumed people only thought of me in those terms."

"For Christ's sake, William!" Dana blurted out them clapped a hand to her mouth. "Sorry William, I shouldn't have blasphemed. I know how much you hate that."

He smiled. "You don't need to apologize to me," He said with a grin as he theatrically rolled his eyes towards heaven. His face grew serious,

"Do I really seem that sanctimonious?"

She was caught off guard by the question, but after a moment, she replied "No, not really. I mean, I know you're a man of deep faith but you're no Bible Thumper and...well...frankly, you're not much of a sinner."

He raised his eyebrows, "So, you think I'm dull?"

She laughed, "Anything but!" She lowered her eyes and said softly, "I think you are a truly noble man...and you do it in such a human way."

He smiled, pleased with her compliment. "So, I'm an eccentric monk living in an Abbey he built for himself! Do you wonder why I have no wife?"

She smiled and shook her head. "Now you're just being factious! You are a famous actor, well to do, with a beautiful home, and quite good looking to boot! Any woman would jump at the chance for a catch like you!"

He chuckled, "Madame, please! You'll make me blush!"

She laughed. "Let's see if I can!

"You are intelligent, worldly, and good with your hands. I still marvel over the latches and window openers whenever I open or close a door in this house. Everything is more clever and unique than I have ever seen anywhere! And none of that includes your railroad or the Aunt Polly!"

He shrugged, looking a bit embarrassed. "Yet, I never thought you were all that impressed with all these trappings. You always seem to take everything in stride."

"Well, it wouldn't do to have me working around here all googly eyed! But I've loved every minute I have worked for you. It just wouldn't be proper to show it."

"Ha! And I thought I was the actor of this residence!"

She shrugged, "All the world's a stage, and we are but actors upon it."

"My word! And she quotes the Bard himself! There are hidden depths to you, Dana.

"So, tell me, what impresses you the most? My home, the railroad, or my houseboat?"

She looked at him seriously for a moment, and then answered. "In truth! None of the above. What I love most about you is how you will go frog hunting with Ozaki whenever you need to replace Mike or Lena. Or the joy on your face when you bring one home. You are not only happy with what you've made, you're thrilled to ride your motorcycle or drive your train around! Your exuberance is infectious to everyone around you! Not many men in your position can find that…little boy's love of life. I think that is incredibly special. Though, I confess I don't understand your love of cats! One or two I can fathom, but we must be up to a dozen by now!"

He laughed and reached over to pat her forearm. "I know they drive you crazy at times and I thank you for your forbearance. The cats…well, they put movement in my life, though I never planned on acquiring so many. I guess it's a kind of addiction I picked up in all those years on stage. My whole life has been filled with noise and movement, swirling around me like a whirlwind I created. My ears were always filled with a calliope and there were lights and props, all played out in halls filled with every aspect of humanity. Even when I lived on the Aunt Polly all those years, when I wasn't performing, there was the ever changing waters below me and the revolving skies above me. When I built this place in all its solidity of stone, I felt like I was ripped out of existence. Exiled into a hell of stillness. My cats give me that movement I so crave. Their constant prowling and antics aren't a distraction for me but more of an aid in concentration. They make this home more alive." He laughed. "I must sound like a madman!"

"No, actually, strange as it may seem, I understand."

As if on cue, a large brown tabby wandered over to sit at the base of William's stool, looked up at him, and meowed. William reached down with his long arm and scratched to top of the feline's head. Then he sat up and flicked a hand. "Now go to bed, François. It's late."

The cat mewed once more then trotted off.

Dana smiled and shook her head. "I admit that I find the beasts annoying at times, when they are underfoot or popping up and scaring me into grey hair but I think I will look at them in a different light now.

"Though, they'll still get the working end of my broom if they get up to any mischief in my kitchen!"

He laughed. "And rightly so! Still, they are delightful company. Pet them once and a while and they love you unconditionally!" he smiled, "Everyone likes to be loved, Dana."

Something passed in her eyes, and she bit her lip softly, as if in a quandary. After a few more sips of coco, she looked at him shyly.

"Speaking of being loved, William...may I ask you a personal question?"

William was set back by the question; he didn't know if the butterflies in his stomach were from dread or anticipation. He focused and answered. "Of course, Dana."

"What is it like? To be famous? To be one of the greatest actors of all time? Be universally loved by all."

He had the grace to look sheepish. "Oh, My! I wouldn't go that far. I've just been more fortunate than most."

"That's not what I've read, William. From both reviewers and critics!"

He leaned forward and smiled. "Forget those hacks! Anyone who gets a free ticket to a good seat can't be trusted with an opinion." Somewhat shyly, he asked, "What is your impression of my work?"

Now it was Dana's turn to look embarrassed. "Well, the truth is, I've never actually seen you perform."

William was confused. "How is that? I recall leaving you tickets to my plays on numerous occasions. You never used them?"

"Actually...I gave them to Father Yemma, at my church. He raffles them replenish our poor box.

"I'm sorry if you're mad, but they really do help those in need."

William's face grew serious. "I'm not mad at you for giving away the tickets, Dana. Though I am a bit disappointed you never attended a show." He narrowed his eyes at her. "The last time I gave you tickets, I asked you the next morning how you liked the play...and you told me enjoyed it."

Her eyes went wide, and she held up a finger. "I did not lie to you!

"You asked me, and I quote, 'Did you enjoy last night?' To which I replied, 'Yes, very much so! It was a delightful evening!'"

She smiled playfully at him, "It's not my fault you didn't know I meant I had a nice hot bath and read a good book by the fire. After all, aren't you supposed to be a detective?"

William squinted at her with one eye and burst out laughing. "Ah! A challenge! Very well."

He sat straighter in his chair and stared out into space for a moment. As he sat still, the features on his face morphed, seemingly growing longer and less defined. Even his ears stuck out a bit more as he lowered his head and said in an upper crust British fashion.

"You keep a snake for some odd reason."
Her eyes bulged.

"You suffer from gout, in your left foot, on rare occasions."

Her jaw dropped.

"Your mother was a southern belle."

Her head snapped back as if she had been slapped.

He smiled and his face returned to normal. "How did I do?"

She was shaking her head in disbelief, yet her eyes were filed with admiration. "I have heard you do your little parlor tricks, entertaining your guests, yet I am still amazed! How did you know all that?"

"Elementary, my dear Dana!" he said with a laugh. "Simple observation and deduction. Like any good...house.... Lady of the House, you have no love for mice. Yet coincidentally after you took that old glass display case I was tossing out; you changed the mousetraps from the lethal variety to ones that trap the rodents. Add that to the tiny fang marks I saw on your thumbs one day and I was fairly certain you were keeping a snake for a pet."

Dana clapped her hands. "Bravo, Sherlock Holmes! I found him when he was just a baby, no bigger than a pencil. Now he's almost five feet long and as thick as your wrist!"

William's head snapped back. "Whatever in the world would possess– "

"Cyrus keeps the mice-and break-ins down" She cut him off, and then stared at him intently. Seriously, how did you know about the Gout? I never told anyone and I'm sure Doc Blum would never tell a soul. Not even my...husband knew!"

William was abashed. "Forgive me if I was invasive, Dana. But I have known for some time.

"You see, I know you have several pairs of the shoes you prefer to work in, and I have noticed, at times, that the left shoe was a size or two larger than the right one. Obviously to make room for a bandage. And I know you to shy away from certain foods, the types that can cause an outbreak of Gout. Now that it is out in the open, I can confess that I always wanted to send you home to rest when I saw the larger shoe."

She tilted her head at him. "Why didn't you?"

He shrugged. "You never complained or even mentioned it and I know you to be a sensible woman, capable of deciding what she can or can't do, so rather than embarrass each other, I kept my peace."

Dana looked at him a long moment and said softly. "You are a sweet and sensitive man, William Gillette. "Now, about my mother..."

William was glowing at her kind words when he barked a laugh. "Easiest of them all! Such a beautiful and gracious woman as yourself could come from any part of the country, but her biscuits could only have come from south of the Mason-Dixon Line! Recipes like that are only passed from Mother to daughter!"

"Close, but not quite. My mother was born and raised in Connecticut. It was my Granny who taught me how to make biscuits. She was born and bred in Tennessee."

"Oh, to be laid low by a single generation!" he pointed out smugly. "I shall have to hang up my deerstalker hat!"

She laughed, then became serious. "What would your Mr. Sherlock Holmes advise me about the letter from my husband?"

William grimaced and took a long sip of his chocolate. Blowing out a long breath, he replied slowly. "Well...Sherlock is notoriously ignorant of affairs of the heart, but I think he might voice one obvious observation. It would be a pity that such a marvelous woman would hide herself from the world...for fear of being labeled."

She snorted. "Easy for him to say. The ladies in my church would lose their minds if I suddenly became a divorcee!"

"Then, they are not worthy of your attention." he replied softly.

She gazed at him for a moment and asked, "Are you?"

He seemed confused. "Am I, what?"

"Worthy of my attention." She responded gently.

He started to reply, then took a large gulp of his drink. He cleared his throat. "I...I would very much like to be."

She reached over and took his hand. "Then you are William."

William looked like a dumbfounded schoolboy, so Dana took pity on him. She withdrew her hand and refilled the cups from the pot next to her.

"So," she said brightly. "Tomorrow is Christmas Eve. What does the script say?"

13

"So," Catherine asked, as they pulled up to the castle the next morning. "Are you ready for another day of manual labor?"

Collin sighed and shut off the engine. Setting the parking brake, he countered. "Are you? You spent a very long time in the bathroom this morning. I...I thought I heard retching."

She glared at him sharply. "I'm fine! Just try to keep up today."

He looked at her sideways. "Usually, I spend Christmas Eve drinking eggnog and singing Christmas carols...but I guess scrubbing toilets will do!"

She smiled at his sickly sweet comment. "Don't worry, darling, in a few days you'll be able to return to your life of luxury!" The smile dropped from her face, and she got out of the car.

Collin didn't like the sound of that and by the time he followed her into the kitchen, his mood was darkening.

"Morning, Children!" Dana greeted them. "Happy Christmas Eve!"

"However, you see it!" Collin groused. "Where's William?"

Catherine was about to scold him for his manners, but Dana had the situation in hand. She eyed him up and down then handed him a steaming mug of coffee. "You can be as grumpy as you want, Collin. But if you speak rudely to me again, you'll wear the next cup!" Catherine nodded fiercely in support. "William received a telephone call, and he took it in the study. He should be right back."

Collin caught a familiar scent and realized she put a splash of whiskey in the coffee. He took a sip and said, "I'm sorry, Dana. I'm...a bit out of sorts this morning. You're a doll."

She saw the look on Catherine's face, then reached over and patted his cheek. "Try to find some joy in the good we're doing for a friend, please?"

Collin scowled. "C'mon! You must hate this as much as me!"

She smiled slyly. "You'd be surprised, young man."

Before he could press her, William rushed into the room. "Ah! You're here. Excellent!" He caught a whiff of Collin's cup and plucked it out of his hands and handed it back to Dana. "Regular coffee, Dana. Collin has to drive."

"Drive where?" he looked at Catherine, who just shrugged.

Before William could explain, Ozaki strolled into the kitchen. He looked behind him and then turned to face the others. "Good! You're all here. I think it is going well, don't you?"

William was about to berate him for breaking character, but Dana cleared her throat loudly and her eyes flickered to the hallway. They all saw the dragon lady step back out of sight. She had obviously followed Ozaki. William made a few discreet hand signals and Ozaki understood he was being watched. He puffed up his chest and barked.

"William, breakfast will be served immediately. Then I want you to send the boy down to ready the train! I will take my guests for a ride this morning. Make sure everything is in working order and the seats are clean!"

"Breakfast is on the way, sir. Yet, there may be a delay in the train ride. I'm sorry, but Collin needs to go to the train station in Chester and...pick up a package."

Ozaki was about to protest, but he saw the look in William's eyes and played along. "Yes...of course, I had forgotten about that in my joy at seeing my family."

Osaki barked, "Very well, we will use the electric engine. You can handle that on your own."

William bowed. "I apologize, sir, but the electric engine will need at least a day to charge. The steam engine is the only option, and I would need a coalman to operate her."

Ozaki sputtered. "Why do I have a train if I can't use it when I want? You should have anticipated this! I--"

"I can handle the coal." Dana cut him off.

"You, Dana? Have you ever feed a steam furnace before?"

She shrugged and jerked a thumb at the stove. "I keep that beast running all day. I'm sure I can handle a train for forty-five minutes."

"Then, it's settled!" Ozaki capped his hands. "William, you will take Mrs. Woods to make ready for our excursion, while Collin goes to the station. Catherine can serve us breakfast." Without further ado, he turned on his heels and walked away. He reached the end of the hallway and into the great room, where the dragon lady pretended to find him.

"Oh! There you are, Ozaki-Sama!" The rest of what she was saying faded as they walked away.

When they were sure that Ozaki, and more importantly, the dragon lady, were out of earshot, Collin confronted his uncle.

"What package am I picking up in Chester? Why can't I ride the train with you?" He flicked a sideways glance at Catherine. "It's the only fun I'm bound to have this Christmas Eve!"

William sighed and put his hands on Collin's shoulders. Looking deeply into his eyes, he said in a serious tone. "I'm sorry Collin, but this is far more important. You're meeting someone at the station, but you must be getting on. She only has a short layover in Chester before her train leaves for Boston."

Collin, confused to the bone, went to question him further but William cut him off sharply.

"Collin! Please! Just do as I ask." He looked at him kindly, "Do this... for me."

Collin loved, and trusted, this man whole-heartedly, so he just nodded and dug the keys to his automobile out of his jacket. He nodded once.

"I'm on my way." He looked at Catherine. "I'll see you when I get back." With that, he turned and skipped back down the stairs and out the door.

Catherine, her eyes smoldering, looked at William. "She? You're sending him to see a woman?"

William, who was watching Collin leave, a concerned look on his face, whirled on her. "Catherine Alexander! Never have I known you to be a blithering idiot-please don't change that now! It will all be...proper and, hopefully, for the best!"

He ended the conversation by turning to Dana and grinning. "I need to change into my engineer outfit. Go over breakfast with Catherine and meet me at the shed in a half hour." The shed being the building where he housed his engine and passenger cars. "Be sure to wear some warm clothes, sturdy boots, and a pair of sturdy gloves."

"My, won't I be quite the sight?" she cooed back at him.

He winked. "You'll still be the prettiest coalman of any rail line in America." They laughed and he headed to the back staircase to his room. He made it two steps before he stopped and turned back towards them. "Err...by the way, have either of you been collecting laundry...in my room?"

The girls looked at each other and shook their heads. Dana asked. "Why do you ask?"

He shrugged. "It's nothing really. I left a piece of clothing on my bed and it vanished." He shook his head and grinned. "No matter. Must be a product of late night Dirty Heinies!"

Dana turned to her friend, who was looking at her strangely. She started giving her instructions before she could ask any awkward questions. "Serve everyone coffee, or tea, first, while the bagels are toasting, then bring them out with the platter I made." Dana gestured towards a large silver platter, loaded with jams, butter, creamed cheese and slices of smoked salmon.

"Then just take the pans out of the oven and put them in the chaffing dishes on the side table. They are all ready and they can serve themselves. There is bacon, ham, eggs, breakfast potatoes, and flap jacks."

Catherine's eyes lit up. "Sounds yummy!" Then her eyebrows furrowed, and she tilted her head, "But really American! Do Japanese people even eat those things?"

"They do when they're in East Haddam. Now, let's get the coffee on the cart."

As they bustled about, collecting everything they needed, Catherine said, in a voice that was trying to be non chalant, "You and Mr. Gillette have been spending a few late nights lately."

Dana stopped and turned to face her. "Never mind about us. How are things with you and Collin? You don't seem as...happy as when you arrived."

Catherine looked at her and tears leaked out of her eyes. "Oh, Dana, I don't know what to think anymore! New York was a dream. I felt like a princess and loved every minute of it! I know Collin loves me and I want to fit into his life. He's quite the man about town." She sighed, "But when we came back, and he had to do some real work...I saw another side to him. I saw how far apart we are. Oh, I know we come from different places in life. I know I was the maid, and he was the rich man's son, but I never saw him that way. It wasn't until we had to work together, did I see the big difference between us." She looked at her friend. "I want us to have what you and John had...at first, at least."

Dana stuck up a hand to cut her off. "No, you don't! John and I are getting a divorce."

Catherine's eyes flew wide open. "When did this happen...How did it happen?"

"There's no time to get into that now, Catherine. You know we've been estranged a long time and he wants to move on with someone else."

"That rat!"

Dana shook her head. "No. He has every right. After talking to William these past few nights, I've come to realize that everyone has the right to be happy! Look, my point is- John wanted me to be the perfect Navy Officer's wife and I wanted him to settle down on the river with me and get a job. I know we loved each other enough to make either way work. We could have been happy. But both of us were too stubborn to bend our necks to change and we ended apart. Don't make the same mistake. Collin may not scrub the tub to your standards, but William tells me he works hard and does extremely well at running his father's theater syndicate. What's important is that he is a good man, and he loves you to the moon and back! You two may not see the world in the same light, but you see each other just fine. He has held out his hand to you. Don't slap it away because it's not calloused!"

Catherine looked at her for a moment then nodded her head. She sighed and said softly, "I'll need both his hands soon enough."

Dana looked at her strangely, but the sound of a tinkling bell stopped her from saying more. The bell paused a moment, then rang incessantly.

Dana jerked her head towards the dining room. "Better get his worship's coffee before he breaks that bell!"

"He better not break it!" Catherine declared as she gripped the coffee cart and began to push it. "I'm planning on beating him senseless with it after this is over!"

14

Collin pulled up to the Chester train station and got out of his car. He walked over and stood on the platform in front of the depot, looking around to see who he might be there to meet. Of course, William, dramatically cryptic as usual, hadn't told him who he was to see.

In a minute or so, a woman approached him and raised a hand in greeting. She was older, yet attractive and well dressed in a blue, billowy pantsuit all the women were wearing these days. Collin was sure he had seen her before.

"Mr. Frohman? Collin Frohman?"

"At your service," he answered. "Don't I know you?"

She smiled. "I'm surprised you remembered. It was ten years ago, and you were just a teenager."

A light went off in Collin's head. He snapped his finger. "You're an actress! You were in 'Secret Service' with my Uncle Will. My father produced that play, and I had a summer job as a grip."

She beamed. "I'm impressed. You have your father's gift for faces," and her expression softened, "You have his good looks too!" She stuck out her hand. "Rita Joilet."

Collin took it yet looked doubtful. "Listen, Miss Joilet, if this is about a job, I'd be happy to talk to you some other time, but right now...I'm in the middle of something..."

"Oh, no, Mr. Frohman, it's nothing like that. In fact, I retired some years ago. William telephoned me out of the blue the other day and when he found out I was passing through today on my way to Boston, he asked me to speak with you. You see, I was on the Lusitania when she was sunk." Her eyes moistened, "In fact, I was the last person to see your father alive."

The blood drained from Collin's face, and he froze inside. She took pity on his state and took him by the arm. "Let's find a place to sit, shall we?"

15

After they had dressed and went out the door, Catherine went about clearing the breakfast dishes from the table. She could feel the old man's eyes on her and whenever she glanced in his direction, he grinned at her like a mad horse. She thought him to be dotty, but harmless all the same. At least, she hoped he wouldn't be too much of a bother.

Catherine wasn't particularly upset about missing the train ride. Mr. Gillette had often given her rides on the rails, and she knew it was as cold as a jilted lover outside. What she did resent was how, earlier, Ozaki ordered her to stay in and watch over the old man.

"Samata-Sama will not be joining us for a ride on my train. He prefers to rest by the fire. Keep it stoked and tend to his every need!" he proclaimed in a pompous tone. He flapped a hand at the dining area. "You may also clean up after breakfast. You should be able to accomplish both by the time we return!" He took his brother by the arm, chatting away in Japanese. The dragon lady stayed back and looked at Catherine with a severe face. She looked her up and down with a critical eye and glanced at her father. Catherine knew she was questioning her ability to watch over her father.

Catherine wanted to kick her in the shin, but she smiled sweetly and gave her a slight curtsey.

"I will care for him as if he were my own Grandfather, Ma'am."

The dragon lady leaned in and sneered. "He had better tell me just that-for your sake!"

Before Catherine could react, the dragon lady spun about and followed the men, chattering like a magpie when she reached then. From sour grapes to peaches and cream in six steps. As the other three were putting on their outercoats, she went over to see the old man who was sitting in a chair.

She leaned down and said, slightly louder than normal. "Is there anything I could get you, Sir?" The old man gazed up at her with rheumy eyes and said something softly in Japanese. Catherine wanted to roll her eyes and sigh. Instead, she responded, "I'm so sorry, Sir, but I don't understand. Do you speak English?"

The old man waggled his eyebrows and smiled. He held out an arm for help getting up. Catherine helped him to his feet, and he shuffled over to the fireplace, leaning slightly on her. Once in front of the fire, he turned and slowly, but gracefully, sank to the floor to sit on the rug, with his legs almost tucked underneath his scrawny behind. She was surprised he didn't break any of his old bones with the move, and then realized the old man had probably sat that way his entire life. Ozaki had once told her that there were very few chairs in his native land, and everyone sat on pillows or mats. The old man laid his cane across his lap and closed his eyes, absorbing the heat. After waiting a moment, Catherine backed away and went to clear the table.

The old man had opened his eyes when she started clearing the table and now his gaze was giving her goosebumps. If he were forty years younger, she would think he was undressing her with his eyes.

The breakfast cart was only half loaded but she wheeled it into the kitchen just to get out of his sight for a moment.

Miss Rita Joilet had led Collin into the small coffee shop in the station and found a booth. Easing into seats across from each other, and still feeling a little shocked at her being on the Lusitania when his father died, he stammered, "How...why..."

Rita looked at him with pity. "If this is too painful for you, Mr. Frohman, we don't have to discuss it. I have no wish to bring you pain, especially on Christmas Eve!"

Collin managed to focus. "No, No, I'm sorry, you caught me off guard. I had no idea what this was about. William never told me who I was meeting -or why!"

"I gathered that when I introduced myself." She tittered and sighed. "William. Ever the drama king!" She shook her head. "Well, he should have warned you! My offer still stands; we can talk about anything else, if you like."

Collin shook his head slowly. "I'd like to hear your story. I've asked many people over the past year, but no one knew anything about my father's last hours. Why haven't you said anything before now?"

She looked away but was saved having to answer right away when the waitress came to take their order. Collin ordered coffee for them both and Rita turned back when the waitress walked away.

"Survivor's guilt, I suppose. I brake down every time, I tried to speak of it. I nearly went mad over the horror of it. It was six months before I could reach out to William and tell him the story. I only forced myself to do so because I knew how close William was to your father and I have great respect for them both." She paused and swallowed. "I have to say, I'm not sure how to explain it to you. It's bad enough to lose a father but to hear the details…"

Collin managed to smile. "Please. I want to know. Start at the beginning and tell me everything!"

Smoke puffed from the train's stack like an angry man smoking a pipe when Dana reached the shed where it was stored. William was in the driver's seat, fiddling with the gears and gages as the engine roared in the enclosed space. He was bundled up for the cold, a great coat over his outfit and thick railroad canvas gloves, though he still wore his engineer's cap. Dana had to shout twice before he noticed her.

He flipped a few switches and pushed a lever, and the engine went into an idle.

"Ah! There you are!" he exclaimed. "I was wondering where you got to. I thought I would pick you up on the way." He reached down and helped her onto the engine. The small area kept them pressed together until William could get her onto a box next to his seat. Gently, he lowered her onto her perch. "There. That's the official coalman's seat."

She looked up at him. "Shouldn't you be showing me what to do before I sit, and we get going?"

He slid into his seat and smiled. "It's already done. There's a good bed of coal. We should have enough steam to make the ride. If not, we just have to throw a few shovels into the boiler. I usually do it myself."

She looked up at him and squinted. "Then why, pray tell, was I roped into this?"

William grinned at her slyly and pulled a few levers. "Hang on!"

The engine lurched backwards, and Dana grabbed William's thigh for support. Once in motion, the ride smoothed out, she removed her hand and said, "You didn't answer my question. Why am I here?"

William looked down at her and grinned. "The ambient air temperature is around thirty-six degrees today. With the wind speed it will feel like zero, or perhaps, below."

Dana grimaced and gave him a hard stare. "All the more reason to answer the question, William!"

William twisted in his seat to look over his shoulder behind him. "This morning, I was doing my best to dissuade Ozaki from taking the train out. I may have been successful..." he paused and looked at her. "If someone hadn't piped up and volunteered to feed the engine."

He winked and deadpanned, "I wouldn't want to deprive you of a good deed over a little discomfort in the cold!"

Dana knew he wasn't a vindictive person. She decided to put him on the spot. "What's the real reason, William!" she asked quietly.

William swallowed and cleared his throat, then shrugged and looked back at the tracks. "You said I should share my passions with someone. Well, this railway is my favorite pastime. I...was hoping you will come to enjoy it as much as I." He cleared his throat again and asked sheepishly. "Am I out of line?"

She smiled up at him. "I'll let you know if we get back alive!"

He looked down at her and waggled his eyebrows. "At least we are prepared and have the boiler box at our feet to stay warm! Our guests will have neither.

"By the time we reach my miniature Penn Station, I suspect our little tyrant will regret having insisted on this run!"

Dana laughed. "Oh, Goody! I love a little torture on Christmas Eve- as long as it's all in good fun!"

William deftly backed the train up to the shed he had designated as Grand Central Station and quickly hooked up the passenger cars. As he returned to his engineer's perch, Dana looked up towards the house.

"What's keeping them?"

"They're not coming here," William scoffed. "Oh, No! The master wants us to pick them up on the platform." He pulled out his watch. "We'll leave in precisely seven minutes." As William fiddled with the gauges and switches, Dana peered closely around the cab. She had ridden in the passenger car a few times before, but this was the first time she was in the driver's seat.

"This is quite a sophisticated piece of machinery, isn't it? I confess, until now, I always thought of the train as a big toy."

William grinned. "And me as a little boy in long pants?"

"Well...you are!" she shot back.

The smile dropped off his face. "You don't think it...ostentatious?"

"No! Of course not! Maybe if you had someone driving you around, but I've never seen you give up your engineer's position yet! You are a little boy in long pants."

William's eyebrows shot up and he grinned. "Is that the only thing?"

She gave him a coy smile and pointed forward. "We'd better move along, William. Mr. Ozaki will have our heads if we're late!"

"But of course!" he said with a flourish as he flipped a switch and pushed the accelerator lever forward. "The Seven Sister Rail Line prides itself on punctuality!" A short way down the line they came to a wooden platform, built next to the tracks. Ozaki, his brother, and the dragon lady were waiting as William brought the train to a stop. After lining the steps up to the passenger car, William climbed down off the engine and greeted Ozaki and his guests. Yukio was much more than impressed.

"Yukitaka, this is amazing. I must confess, when you first told me about it, I thought it must be nothing more than a child's toy. Yet this is an actual train! Where did you get this? What is its top speed? How far do the tracks go?"

Ozaki puffed up like a peacock. "The tracks extend for three point two miles where we shall reach another station. One I named 'Penn Station". Do you know the reference, 'Penn Station'? There we can turn around for the return trip. Please allow William to explain my railroad. I trained him myself."

William managed to keep a straight face and went on to tell where the train was built and how long it took to lay the tracks and build the station. He went into the specifics of the engine and cars, but Ozaki cut him off.

"Enough William! My brother doesn't need to know every detail! We're here to give him a ride- not sell him the damn thing! It's cold! Let us be on our way!" Blank faced, but fuming inside, William bowed slightly and helped them up into the first car behind the engine.

"Take us along the river first, William." Ozaki ordered imperiously. He turned to his brother. "The train has a bit over three miles of track that meander, and the view of the river is magnificent. Especially this time of year when there are no leaves on the trees."

The passengers were chatting away, Ozaki pointing out landmarks as William climbed back into his seat. Soon they were chugging down the tracks, at a quarter throttle, hugging the side of the hills that sloped down to the river. True to Ozaki's description, the views of the river were spectacular from their rolling perch on high. The ground and the tree skeletons were covered with a pristine coat of snow, giving the dark blue waters of the Connecticut River a perfect backdrop. The dragon lady nearly screeched with excitement as she spotted a pair of bald eagles soaring just above the water in search of prey. They cheered with gusto when one of the birds suddenly dropped into the water and emerged with a fish squirming in its talons.

William looked over to see what Dana's reaction was, but she was not looking at the river but the high rock wall that lined the right side of the track. "What's so fascinating, Dana?"

She looked up at him, wide eyed. "It's incredible William! All the other times I rode this train, I was looking at the river view. Sitting up front here, I have a closer look at the tracks and I can appreciate the time and work it took to lay these rail beds. It is one hell of an engineering feat!"

He smiled. "And that's one of the things I love about you, Dana. You see the big picture."

"Why did you go to these lengths? Cutting into the side of the hill was a lot of effort. Why not just lay the tracks along the top?"

"I designed the lay-out to keep the tracks as level as possible. Everything was built to that end. The more level- the faster I can go." He took a pair of earmuffs out of his coat and handed them to Dana, then took out another and bade her to put them on.

"My ears aren't cold yet."

He winked at her. "They're not to keep the cold out."

16

The old man had not stirred for a half an hour, so Catherine assumed he had fell asleep, sitting by the fire. He was content enough, so she went about cleaning the dining room and kitchen. When she emerged from the kitchen, the old man was still in the same place. 'He must be stiff as a board by now', she thought to herself. She walked over to see that he was alright.

When she was directly in front of him, the geezer's eyes popped open, and he grinned at her from ear to ear. Catherine smiled back and curtseyed.

"Can I get you anything? A pillow or a cup of tea?" Then she felt foolish as he most likely didn't understand a word she said.

He answered her in Japanese, so rapid she could not discern one word from the next. She shook her head to show him she did not understand, but the old man was not put off. He reached up with one arm and gestured for her to sit. Confused, but not wanting to insult the man, she tucked her dress under her and sank to her knees, the shifted her rump on to the rug with her legs curled to the side. The old man was delighted, and he began to become more animated as he jabbered away and smiled at her like a loon. It seemed to make the old man happy, and she decided she could use a break, so she smiled back at him, nodding on occasion as if she understood. The old man suddenly finished with a flurry and began to rise to his feet. She sprang up and the old man held out an arm for her to take. Gesturing with his cane to the upstairs balcony, he began to shuffle towards the stairs.

"Oh, you're ready for nap, are you? Alright then, let's get you up to your room." The old man smiled up at her and waggled his eyebrows.

The coffee was delivered, and the waitress departed. Rita added some cream and sugar then slowly stirred the cup. Spoon still in hand, she looked up at Collin and began.

"As you already know, I'm an actress. That year, I was contracted to do one of your father's productions in England. I knew your father from some other plays I had been in, but only on a professional level. I was only one of a gaggle of young actresses that the syndicate booked passage for on the Lusitania. I didn't even know your father was on the ship. He was in first class, and we were not. At first, the trip was an absolute gas! We all had a grand time. We had the run of the ship, and every night was a party. One night I got so swizzled that my friends had to carry me down to my cabin to sleep it off." She looked slightly embarrassed after the admission.

Collin grinned to put her at ease. "I do that once a month on average!"

"I was out like a light when the first torpedo hit us and was just opening my eyes when the second one knocked me out of my bunk. I stumbled to my feet, head pounding and stomach rolling over, and the sirens began to wail. I stumbled over to the porthole but all I could see was thick black smoke. My panic threw the hangover into the back seat. The lights went out and I stumbled about, trying to get dressed. Then I heard the calls to abandon ship and I spent God knows how long trying to pack a bag of everything I thought I needed. Eventually, I got out of my cabin and stepped right into bedlam.

People were running up and down the passageway, screaming names and knocking each other over. I managed to make my way to a staircase I knew led up to the observation deck. It was eerily empty, so I started up. When I was about halfway up the steep staircase, the ship lurched again, and I was thrown down the steps. I must have hit my head because when I opened my eyes there was a man leaning over me, calling my name and wiping my face with a cloth. It was your father. 'Mr. Frohman,' I said, 'What the hell is going on?'

He helped me to my feet and looked me straight in the eye. 'I'm sorry, Miss Joilet, but it's too late in the day for anything but the blunt truth. The ship is sinking. We don't have too much time left.'

"I grabbed him by the lapels and said, 'We have to get to a lifeboat!' He shook his head sadly. 'They are already gone. There are none left.' I started to cry, and he took me gently by the arm and said, 'We are heading to the upper deck. Why don't you join us?'

I noticed then there was another man and together, they helped me up a few sets of stairs until we reached the top of the boat. When we stepped out into the open air, I realized how dire our situation was! I could see that the ship was extremely low in the water and the sea was rising fast. Men were jumping off into the water and there were several lifeboats all rowing away from the ship. The deck was at an incline and Charles led us up to the stern where we found an open space to stand. Moments later another man climbed up to us, a ship's officer, and we stood in a circle. 'How long?' your father asked, and the man replied, 'Hard to say...but soon.'

The other man with your father, I later found out it was Alfred Vanderbilt, shrugged and said to your father, 'It doesn't look good, Charles.' Your father smiled back at him and replied, 'What is death, but life's most glorious and greatest final adventure?'"

Collin nodded. "That's a line from the Peter Pan production. My father loved that production."

"Oh, I always wondered. Your father produced a flask and cigars and passed them around. The officer looked at me and asked, 'Why did you not get on a lifeboat ma'am?' Your father, grinning like the devil's imp answered for me. 'The lady was taking a nap. Such beauty won't allow a little sinking to interfere with that!'

We laughed at the sally, and then I asked, 'Why didn't you two get on a lifeboat?' It occurred to me that two men of such wealth and prestige could surely have secured a place of safety. Mr. Vanderbilt shrugged and replied, 'When the bar cleared out, I thought I would stay for a quiet drink.' Then your father added, 'I tried to pull the geezer off his stool, but this bum knee of mine slowed me down.'

I couldn't believe there were so cavalier. The ship's officer laughed with them, then told me,

'Don't you believe a word from them, Miss. When everyone else was running over each other to get to the boats, these gentlemen went down to steerage to show folks how to make Moses' baskets for the little ones.' Then he stiffened and saluted. 'It is my honor to stand with them now!'

'Bah!' your father replied. 'Hand me my flask and I'll drink to that!'

I was grateful to your father for sparing me the indignity of recounting my clumsiness. I watched him as he took a swig from his flask and puffed away on his last cigar like he didn't have a care in the world. I leaned close to him and asked. 'How can you be so calm? I'm scared enough to wet myself!'

He laughed, 'I wouldn't bother, if I were you. We'll be wet soon enough.'

I couldn't believe he was still joking, as now the water wasn't too far away from our feet. 'Aren't you even scared?'"

He smiled and took the last swig from his flask then tossed it into the water. He threw his cigar in after it, took me by the hands, and locked eyes with me. 'Rita, I came from nothing and have more than I ever dreamed of. God has given me the absolute best of life. A loving, steadfast wife, a son I love with all my heart to carry on my name, and the very best friend a man could ask for! I've accepted these gifts from God and enjoyed every minute of them. How could I not accept God's will now? I will put my fate in his hands and I'm sure everything will be just as it should be!'

Rita wiped a tear from her eye and went silent for a moment. Collin let her be for a moment, and then prompted, "What happened then Rita?"

She snapped out of her reverie and said, "Not a moment later, a huge wave crashed over us and swept us from the deck. I was tumbled and tossed about but I somehow came to the surface. I clung to a piece of flotsam for a while before one of the lifeboats came upon me and I was pulled into the boat until we were rescued. I never saw your father or the other men again. I was the only one from our group that survived."

Easing the acceleration lever forward the train began to pick up speed. Soon it was chugging along at nearly twenty miles an hour, which was about two thirds of its top speed. The increase wasn't as noticeable on the solid train bed, but when they crossed over a short bridge that spanned a walking trail the wheels clacked in rapid succession, highlighting their velocity.

As they passed through a wooded section of the route, the tracks straightened out and William, grinning like a madman, pushed the lever all the way to the stop. A wooden trestle, nearly one-hundred and twenty-five feet long, that raised them over the low-lying marshlands, loomed ahead of them. The train shot like an arrow across the span, the engine and cars it pulled swaying with the give and take of the wood supports. They were over the long trestle in just under a minute, and then the tracks veered to the left and the train's balance shifted to the right.

Dana grabbed William's knee in a panic, with both hands as she felt herself pulled outward. William's arm shot out and she felt the comfort of his hand on her shoulder, pulling her tight to him. The contact pleased her greatly and when she looked up at him, she could see he felt the same. William kept his face forward, and she threw a glance back over her shoulder to see how the passengers were doing. Ozaki's brother had a white-knuckle grip on the side of the cab but his face was stoic. The dragon lady on the other hand, looked all put out. Her face was white as a ghost and her gaudy make-up made her look like a caricature. A terrified one. Ozaki was shouting something angrily at William's back, but either he didn't hear or was unwilling to acknowledge. Suddenly, something Ozaki saw caused him to clamp his mouth shut and sit back quickly. Dana returned her gaze forward and saw why.

The train was hurtling towards a dark hole in the side of a hill.

Though Dana had been through the tunnel at full speed before on her previous rides, being up front gave it an entirely different perspective. She trusted William but gripped his knee even harder. He laughed and squeezed her tighter. She lifted off her earmuffs to hear Ozaki shouting at William to slow down and then back at the dragon lady in Japanese. She assumed he was trying to reassure them there was no danger.

Apparently, the message didn't get through to the dragon lady and she let out a scream as they shot into the blackness of the tunnel. William had purposely designed it with a curve so no light would shine through until they reached the other side. They burst into sunlight then hit another curve that caused the train to sway like a drunken sailor. They zipped through some wooded areas then William was forced to slow down as they reached the turnaround at the end of the line he had dubbed, 'Penn Station'. As soon as they were at walking speed. Ozaki climbed forward from the passenger car and whacked William in the shoulder with his hat.

"Just what do you think you're doing?" he hissed in William's ear. These are my family-not one of your theater trollops! Are you trying to frighten them to death? You...You...blithering idiot!"

William looked forward as innocently as he could. "I beg your pardon, sir. I was just trying to give your guest a ride they would remember."

"Huh!" Ozaki grunted. "They'll remember it alright! I imagine they will have nightmares! Now slow down for the return trip! No more than half throttle! I want them to enjoy the scenery and not be turned into icicles!" Ozaki turned to go back to his seat and saw his relatives looking at him. He turned back to William and shouted. "Fool! Keep this train in control or I will run it myself and you can walk back to the Castle!"

Osaki sat back down next to his brother and they both spoke soothingly to the woman to calm her down. Dana had to bend down and open the boiler door to hide her giggling. She tossed a few chunks of coal into the fire with her free hand and looked up to see William turning red-faced as he tried to hold his laughter back. Even though William had slowed their speed to a crawl as they wound their way around the turnaround, neither one broke contact.

A short way on the return trip and they reached a round stone column off to the side that was fifteen feet tall and nearly ten feet wide. Here the tracks split off and they could either return the way they came or take the tracks to the left that would take them through another section of the property. Ozaki called out to William and ordered him to go left. William sighed and brought the engine to a halt. He had to jump off and manually switch the rails, which he did smoothly with all the practice that he had. Dana kept the boiler full and quickly they were heading down the tracks- at a much slower pace.

"I don't know why he wants to come this way," he groused. "It may be scenic when the foliage is on the trees but it's just a boring ride through a dull vista in the winter! Worse so, at this pace!"

"Oh, stop complaining!" Dana chided him. "You had your fun!" She giggled and added, "I wish Catherine and Collin were here to see their faces! Besides, I think the snow is beautiful, the way it sparkles in the sun."

William looked down at her and smiled. "You're right. And no route could be boring with such fine company."

Dana smiled at the compliment, then slowly grew somber. "Unfortunately, the ride, like our little rouse, will only last a short while." Then she fell silent and looked away. William sensed a change in her mood but let it go for the moment. He had an idea why she was quiet but needed some time to put his own thoughts together.

After ten minutes of riding through the trees, the tracks led along a large pond. Snow covered and with a lot of wild growth on the edges, the middle had patches of ice where the snow had blown off. Ozaki called for a halt and William brought the train to a stop. He stood to see what Ozaki wanted, but the little man called out.

"Stay where you are and keep the engines warm. I just want to show my brother the pond." He had Yukio climbed down off the car and Ozaki began to point out various features in Japanese. The dragon lady stayed in her seat, looking miserable, hunched over in her seat. Neither William nor Dana were inclined to ask her if she needed anything.

17

Catherine helped the old man up to his room and was going to leave him at the door, but the old man clung to her and tugged her into the room. Jabbering away at her, he had her sit on the bed before he toddled off the bathroom. Catherine wasn't sure what was going on and was trying to be respectful, but there was no way she was going to wipe his bum or tuck him in for a nap. As soon as he came out of the bathroom, she was going back to work.

The door swung open in a few minutes and Catherine nearly choked on her heart, when she saw the old man standing in the doorway, wearing only his socks and licking his lips at the sight of her.

Mortified, she slammed her eyes shut and turned her head as he shuffled towards the bed, speaking in in a low, crooning tone. She nearly jumped out of her skin when she felt his hand on her arms, gently trying to nudge her towards the bed, still croaking his obvious enticement.

Her eyes flew open to see his grinning face not an inch from her breasts. The realization of his intentions made her want to crack him a good one, but she was brought up to respect the elderly. She shook off his hand and took a step back, furious.

"Why...You old goat!"

He was amused by her reaction and began to cackle like a hen.

At her limit of patience, she turned on her heels and went out the door. Before she slammed it shut, she barked into the room. "Put your clothes on and act your age!"

As the two brothers began to walk around the pond, Dana looked up at William, her eyes wet with moisture. William recoiled a bit in surprise and asked, "Whatever is the matter?"

"I'm not sure I can work for you anymore!" Then she rushed inside. "Everything has changed. Before, you were my employer, and I was your cook. We knew our places...and held our feelings in check! Now that I've gotten to know you, I don't know if I can stay in those boundaries."

"Yes, our relationship has changed...but for the better," William paused and added gently, "don't you think so?"

Still dubious, she nodded.

"Besides, I never thought of you as just 'the cook and housekeeper'. You have been the lady of the house ever since you first step foot in the door. Without Catherine and you, it would have been just a big pile of stone with a couple of grumpy old bachelors puttering around. You are what gave the rocks and wood warmth and life! And now that our little bird, Catherine, has flown the coop, we...I... need your feminine touch even more! If you were to leave us, I'd have to tear this castle down and start all over!"

She laughed, "Now you're just making fun of me."

"No, I mean it!" He looked at her wide-eyed and straight faced. "Truth is, Dana, I don't want to waste another minute with our old attitudes. If I had known your...situation before this week, I'm certain we would have connected on another level years ago." He reached down and squeezed her hand on his knee. "For a man who has mimicked Sherlock Holmes a thousand times, I was a fool not to investigate our feelings for each other before now! You say I should share my life with someone special." He grinned at her sheepishly. "I am."

Dana's cheeks colored slightly and she smiled from ear to ear.

William's demeanor changed and he sighed dramatically. "Yet, what would a beautiful and intelligent woman see in an old codger like me? Alas, for I am in the dregs of age!"

Dana elbowed him gently. "Save your malarkey for the stage! I know you, William Hooker Gillette! True, you do carry a good amount of experience, but I have seen you racing about on your motorcycle or wading through this pond looking for frogs with Ozaki! Or better yet, we are sitting on the testament of your boyish heart. Like Granny says- 'Time doesn't age a man-wasting time does!' And you waste very little that I can see! No, I stick by my previous statements. Any woman would be happy by your side. I know I would."

William beamed, "Oh, Dana, we shall-"

"William!" Ozaki's bellow cut him off. Dana and William had not noticed that the brothers had returned to their seat. "What's going on up there? Stop canoodling and get this train moving. It's cold!

Take us directly to Grand Central. We wish to get inside as soon as possible!"

William waved in acknowledgement, blew the whistle a few times, and set the train back in motion. In minutes he had her up to half speed. Dana lifted off her perch and spoke in his ear. "Thank you, William. I have really enjoyed this ride."

"I hope you will enjoy many more..., Dana."

She sat back down and smiled up at him.

"I believe I shall." Then she added, "As long as you let me drive once and a while!"

William laughed. "I believe this day merits an extra-large Dirty Heinie!"

18

Dana was watching William and enjoying the smile on his face, when he suddenly stiffened and peered ahead. Dana could see the train shed up ahead, but it was a few minutes before she could make out a figure waiting by the entrance. She was surprised to see it was Inspector Rowan again. Holding his hat in one hand and another telegram in the other.

William's eyes flew open in concern. Rowan could ruin the entire scheme unwittingly. Dana was irked.

"Another telegram?" she whispered to William. "Is that fool going to pester me to death? I already signed the papers and sent them off!"

William forgot all about the act for a moment. "You signed the divorce papers?" She smiled and shrugged her shoulders.

"Sorry. Your cook is now a fallen woman!" She patted his knee. "I suppose I should have told you that...but, like Granny says, 'Don't bring out the cow if they only want some milk.'"

William laughed. "I want the whole farm! And you are not 'fallen'. You are free to find your own happiness now!"

She looked back at him coyly, "I'm thinking it won't be much of a search..."

As soon as the train stopped, Rowan was about to call out. William pulled the whistle to drown out his greeting, and then jumped off the train to intercept Rowan. The two carried on a quick, but quiet conversation, and then William said loudly. "Certainly, Chief Inspector! Allow me to help them disembark."

As soon as the passengers were off, the dragon lady excused herself. "Forgive me if I go ahead to the house. I need to...freshen up."

William and Dana watched her scurry up the path in small mincing steps, nearly cross-legged. Dana leaned in and whispered to William. "I hope she can 'freshen up' before she wets herself!" Then she sighed and held out her hand to take the telegram from Rowan.

Catherine heard the train pull up outside, yet nearly jumped out of her shoes when the French doors to the veranda suddenly shot open and the dragon lady burst into the great room. Catherine regained her composure and was about to talk to her about her father's behavior, but the woman ignored her completely and hustled over to the stairs and up to the bathroom, slamming the door behind her.

Catherine felt her anger swell inside her as she waited for someone to appear so she could complain when she saw the dragon lady reappeared and made a beeline across the room to her. Catherine pointed a finger in the general direction of the old man's room and said fiercely, "That old goat tried to...He's disgusting!"

The dragon lady shot her a dirty look then ducked into her own room, slamming the door behind her. Appalled, Catherine stamped her feet and went down to the great room to wait for the men. Ruse or no ruse, they were going to get an earful from her! Moments later, the dragon lady came down the stairs and walked up to Catherine. Arms crossed over her chest, Catherine barked at the woman.

"I don't know how things work in the Japan," she started, "but I wasn't raised to be pawed at by some dirty old leech! You had..."

Catherine's head snapped to the side when the woman backhanded her across the face. "Where is my scarf, you cow? Give it back or I will beat you within an inch of your life!"

Catherine didn't have a clue as to what she was talking about and didn't care. Her eyes blazed and she threw a looping punch in response. But the dragon lady was quicker. She grabbed Catherine's wrist in her right hand and twisted, driving Catherine down to one knee. Her left arm cupped Catherine's elbow and she applied pressure. Catherine screamed.

Rowan walked right past Dana with the telegram and approached the two Japanese men, who were looking at him oddly. Each for different reasons. Rowan stopped in front of Ozaki and bowed slightly. "Good afternoon, Mr. Ozaki. I'm sorry to bother you on Christmas Eve." He turned to Yukio and said, "I presume you are Yukio Ozaki? I received a call from the Governor's office earlier and was instructed to see you got this right away."

Yukio bowed and took the paper. Rowan tipped his hat and walked away. As he passed

William and Dana, he slowed and said out of the corner of his mouth. "This story, I have to hear sometime soon! Merry Christmas you two!"

Yukio opened the paper and read it slowly. A crestfallen look on his face, he turned to his brother. "I'm afraid we must cut our visit short, Brother. I have to get back to Washington immediately!" He looked back at the paper. "It seems that they are stopping the express from Boston at the Chester station, just to pick us up. It will be there at five o'clock." As one, all three men pulled out their pocket watches.

He stuffed the paper into his pocket and said to Ozaki. "It is three now. Could we have a word, in private, before I leave?"

"Certainly," Ozaki replied. "Is everything alright, Yukio?"

"Our... the ambassador is failing quickly. He has been fighting the Spanish flu for some time. It is feared he may not make it through the night. I must go to him at once."

Ozaki bowed, "Of course, Yukio. I am sorry we must separate again so quickly." He bowed deeply again. "I am sorry for our ambassador also."

Yukio talked a stream of Japanese and Ozaki replied in the same language, shaking his head emphatically. Yukio looked grave and Ozaki was clearly agitated.

Dana leaned into William and whispered, "I'm thinking Ozaki doesn't like what his brother's telling him!"

William grimaced. "This is no time to slip up now! He must stay in character!"

Ozaki, visibly distressed, spat out a long harangue, then bowed deeply. Yukio sighed then stared down at him for a moment and shrugged. "Karma."

The somber moment was broken by a piercing scream from the castle.

19

After seeing Rita to the train, Collin sat in his car and the tears came. Not so much for sadness, but for pride and love of his father. Each drop drained another bit of the anger and resentment he had carried for the past year. The story he had just heard taught him something important. His father still guided him. He knew now that money and power meant nothing compared to doing the right thing. His father had chosen to help the less fortunate in his final hours. Surely a few more survived because of his sacrifice. How could he resent that? Also, his anger at God melted away. If his father could keep his faith facing death, Collin could keep his facing life.

With a smile, he wiped his face and put the car in gear. He flew down the back roads as he raced back to the castle. The big car was still rocking from his screeching halt by the front entrance, when he flung open the door and jumped out. He ran through the front door and was leaping up the steps to the great room, his heart full of joy, when he heard Catherine's scream. His thoughts stopped when he saw the dragon lady, looming over Catherine and hurting her. He bolted across the room, leaping over the couch, to pull the dragon lady off Catherine and push her away.

"Are you alright, darling?" he asked, helping Catherine to her feet.

The dragon lady sneered at him. "Oh! So, the driver has feelings for the maid, eh?"

Collin glared at the dragon lady with a protective arm around Catherine and balled up fist on his free hand. "Actually, I'm madly in love with her. If you ever touch her again, I will knock you on your keister!"

Enraged, the dragon lady went into a crouch and yanked a hair comb from the bun on her head. The three tines were six inches long, made of steel, and razor sharp. She held it confidently and moved towards the two of them.

Hearing the scream, the three men rushed up the steps to the house and William threw open the French doors that led to the great room. With Yukio and Ozaki right behind him, he dashed into the room. He only got a few steps in, when he came to a halt, as if he ran into a wall. He looked the situation over and his brain processed four facts.

Catherine was crying and rubbing her arm that dangled from her side. Collin stood in front of her, fists raised and weaving from side to side. The dragon lady was in some sort of martial arts stance and waving a weapon at the two of them. And a wrinkled, naked old man was standing up on the second-floor balcony, seemingly cheering Miko on.

The two Japanese men ran around either side of William and Yukio leapt for his sister-in-law. He stepped between Collin and her, facing her and shouted, "Are you mad?" He growled at her in Japanese, and she stepped back and stuck the comb back in her hair.

Ozaki, confused by the scene and angry for it, screamed at the couple, "What is the meaning of this?"

By then, Dana had caught up to them and stood by William's side when Catherine exploded.

"There is no meaning to all this! First, that old goat," she pointed up at the balcony, and then quickly looked away. Dana followed her finger, and then buried her face in William's arm after catching a glimpse of the naked old man, trying to stifle a laugh as Catherine continued. "Tried to...tried to... have his way with me! Then this woman accused me of stealing and slapped me! I tried to defend myself and she nearly broke my arm. Then when Collin came to help me, she threatened to stab us both!"

The dragon lady looked to her brother-in-law and saw no support in his eyes, so with great crocodile tears, she rushed over to Ozaki. "Ozaki-Sama! Please forgive my father, I'm sure he only meant to honor the ugly girl with an afternoon pillow." She drew herself erect and pointed a finger at Catherine, eyes blazing, "But that cow stole my Obi! It was the one with the most beautiful blue herons. I just washed it before we left this morning and I draped it over the chair in my room to dry. When we returned-it was missing! She was the only one in the house! When I confronted her, the boy interfered. He attacked me!" She glared at the two. "They must be in on it together! You should whip them both until they confess!" She ended her speech with a puppy dog look at Ozaki. There was silence in the room for a minute...

Then Ozaki erupted. "How dare you? Even as an honored guest in my house, you have no right to assault this woman and falsely accuse her of theft! I will not hear another word from you!"

Ozaki turned away from her dismissively and went over to put a hand on both Collin and Catherine. He began to apologize profusely to them. The dragon lady looked shocked, then insulted, as Yukio stepped up to her and barked at her with a menacing tone in their native language. As he went on, her eyes widened, then she nodded, and was soon bowing to punctuate his every sentence. He gave a final command and waved a hand at her. She turned and fled up the stairs to pack and ready her father for travel.

Yukio walked over to Ozaki and the couple. He bowed deeply to Catherine and Collin. "My family shames me." They both assured Yukio they didn't hold him responsible in any way. He shrugged. "In any case, I told her to pack her things, then dress and pack her father. We must be ready to leave shortly."

He looked over to William, who hadn't moved. "William, would you be so kind as to call us a cab?"

William bowed slightly, "Of course, sir. Right away."

Yukio turned back to his brother. "Perhaps we can have that word in private now? Come up to my room with me and we can talk while I pack."

Ozaki nodded and they started for the stairs.

Collin took Catherine in his arms and kissed her soundly. He was in a remarkably good mood for what had just transpired.

"Come with me, Catherine! I need to talk to you!" Dazed, Catherine let him lead her away.

That left just Dana and William standing in the great room. Dana looked up at him and with a soft tone and said "Care for that 'Dirty Heinie now? Or do you think it's too early?"

William shook his head ruefully, "Yesterday wouldn't be too early. Let me call for a taxi and I will meet you in the kitchen."

20

Collin kept a protective arm around Catherine as he led her through the dining area and into the conservatory. He closed the doors behind him and set her on the edge of the frog pool below the waterfall. He stood in front of her and asked. "Are you alright? I'm glad I got there when I did."

She looked up at him, slightly irritated. "Just say why you brought me here Collin. I know it must be serious, you walked right past the liquor to get here!"

She gave him a grim stare. "Who was the woman you met?"

He smiled an impish grin. "My Uncle Will is one sharp cookie!" He went on to retell the story that Rita Joliet had told him. When he finished, Catherine smiled sadly and nodded.

"I'm not surprised. Remember, I knew William's best friend Charles Frohman before I knew you! He was a special man." She cocked her head. "You don't seem angry talking about him now."

"I'm not. I've been acting like a spoiled brat, and I won't dishonor his memory that way anymore. Sure, I still loath the people responsible for his death, but I am proud of the way he met his end and the caring for others throughout his life! And I'm not mad at God anymore. I see what my father meant by being blessed and in the end, you must take the bad with the good. If he could be at ease with God when facing his death, how can I do less with my own life?"

Catherine smiled and put a hand on his cheek. "Oh, Collin, that's wonderful. A person needs faith, or they will be lost in this crazy world." She kissed him on the cheek.

Emboldened, he went on, "Look, I know I gave you, and everyone else, a hard time these last few days but you helped me realize something. A man needs to be self-reliant and stay grounded. Sure, it's nice to have money and things, but in the end, it's how you act that you'll be remembered. Money can make living easy, but there is no real life without love!"

He slid off the stones onto one knee before her and took her hands in his. "Catherine Marie, from this moment forward, I will try my best to see what's really important. Can you forgive me?""

Tears gushed from her eyes as a smile split her face. She fell into him and kissed him soundly. When they came up for air, she said, "Yes! There's nothing to forgive. And I promise to appreciate all the advantages you have given me!" She smiled , "Despite your money, good looks, and prestige, I know there is a good man in there!"

His eyes went wide, and his mouth formed an O. "Alright then, and I promise, when we get a home, I will let you do all the cooking and cleaning to your heart's content. No servants!"

Catherine pursed her lips and looked sideways. "Well...perhaps one or two...from time to time." Then she grew mock serious and tapped his nose with a finger. "And we will raise our kids and we'll teach them to catch frogs and clean a fish."

She laughed, "Of course, I'll have to teach you first!"

He smiled with love in his eyes, "How about we teach them to love others and to love God." He looked ponderous, "Besides, I'm not without some talents. When they're old enough, I can teach them to smoke and how to make a good martini and drive Cadillacs, and trains, and...." Collin's lovely rant was overtaken by Catherine's joyous laughter.

Ozaki followed his brother into the guest room and his brother shut the door behind him. Ozaki was uneasy about what was on his brother's mind. He wasn't about to bring up the subject of what had just transpired, and he was sure his brother wouldn't either. Shutting away embarrassing situations was the Japanese way.

"I am so sorry you were summoned, Yukio, it's too bad you have to cut this visit short. I was looking forward to spending Christmas with you."

Yukio picked up a pair of trousers and began to fold them slowly and carefully. Without looking at Ozaki, he replied. "Well... I'm sure William will be happy to have his home back for the holidays."

If Ozaki was shocked, angry, or ashamed, he did not show it. He sighed, "Ah, Yukio! I never could fool you, even when we were children." Suddenly he sat on the bed and put his head down. He looked up, his eyes pleading, "Please, Brother! Please don't let on to William. His acting is everything to him! It would break his heart to know you saw through him!"

Yukio turned to him. "But I didn't see through him! Not really! I did have the fortune to see William perform in England last year. One doesn't forget an actor of his caliber. He was impeccable as the butler these past few days. Don't fear, I will not ruin his performance. Why would I? In my secret heart, I will always cherish the honor of being the audience to a private play by him!"

Ozaki nodded then sighed. "Still, I am ashamed. I'm sorry I lied to you, over the last two days and in all the letters I sent you over the years. I was just so proud you Yukio. You have become a man of great influence. You were the mayor of Tokyo! You have shaped our government from the highest levels. You are here in America because you are the senior envoy of our diplomats. When the cherry trees blossom every spring in Washington, people will sing your praises for years to come." Tears shone in his eyes. "You walk among the Gods, brother, and I am but a servant. I have no honor." Elbows on his knees, Ozaki leaned forward and buried his face in his hands.

Yukio stared down at him for a moment, then sat on his haunches in front of him. Taking Ozaki's hands gently in his, he pulled them away and held them. "You say you have no honor. You are wrong, Yukitaka. My life was dictated from my birth. I was groomed, trained, and punished into the role I was expected to play. Looking back on my life, if given a choice, I would not have involved myself in politics. Any rewards I received from it, I am thankful, however the disappointments have far outweighed the accomplishments! I have had a good life, but it is the life of a bird in a cage."

He looked his brother in the eye and went on. "But you...you were the bird that flew! When father banished you to America, many thought you wouldn't survive. They said you were too proud... too rash! But I knew they were wrong. I knew you were strong and steadfast and that you would endure. You have learned their language and their ways and made a good life for yourself! That much I know is true. Perhaps you do not own this place, but it is obvious to me that you are a big part of it none-the-less! You say you have no honor? Well, I know that is not true! I have known men, great men, and I have met many thousands of others in my travels. I held the power over millions and garnered great influence..." he paused and said clearly, "And yet, I can think of no one who would have done what your friends have done for you! None in our family also. And when I revealed I knew about you and William exchanging roles, you were more concerned with William's feelings than of your own. That is Honor, brother, and you are truly what a Samurai should be!" After a moment, he smiled and winked. "This will be our little secret, forever. Let's have no more talk of it."

Ozaki beamed back at him and stood. Yukio rose and they embraced. Yukio grew somber and asked softly, "Are you sure you won't come with us to see...the ambassador, before he joins our ancestors?"

Ozaki considered it for a moment, then shook his head. "It is better I do not. The past is meant to be left behind."

Having said that, he straightened out his jacket and smoothed out his trouser legs. "I shall send

William up to fetch the baggage. That will please him greatly."

Yukio chuckled. "I'm glad. I promise to be suitable haughty to him." They both laughed and Ozaki headed for the door, but Yukio stopped him with one more question. "If your butler is the greatest Actor in America, who are the others?"

Ozaki laughed. "Well, Mrs. Woods is actually our cook and the maid, Catherine, was actually our maid until she became involved with our chauffer, Collin, who is actually Collin Frohman, owner of the Theater Syndicate."

"Frohman? He is the son of Charles Frohman. I met his father several times when I attended the theater in years past.

"Eeee, he is as rich as the emperor! Your payroll must be to the moon!"

21

    There was too much luggage for just William to handle, so Dana gave him a hand. They were both grateful that Collin and Catherine were out of sight. They passed the bags over to the cabbie and returned to the house to watch Ozaki say his good-byes. The old man they stuffed into the car right away, and after a deep bow to Ozaki, the dragon lady scampered in and sat next to the old man. Yukio and his brother embraced, and then he too got in the car. Ozaki watched them until they rounded a bend and was out of sight. He turned and slowly walked back towards the house.

    Collin and Catherine came into the kitchen as William and Dana sat back down at the counter. Catherine looked at Dana and asked, "Are they gone yet? We thought we heard a car outside."

    "Don't worry," she answered. "The coast is clear. Ozaki just saw them off."

    "Good – Thank God!" Collin said, still grinning ear to ear. "Where's Ozaki. I have a thing or two to say about his family!" He put an arm around Catherine.

    "After he explains my painting and my finest wines!" William warned.

    Ozaki entered the kitchen, and they all drew a great breath to rip into him but choked off their words when William held up a hand for silence. He looked worriedly at his friend.

    Ozaki stood a few paces away from them, still as a statue and had a face like one. William knew something was wrong. In a low but clear voice, Ozaki said, "I will be eternally grateful for all that you have done for me these past few days. You are truly wonderful people." He looked up at them and intoned, "I am honored to be back with my family."

That took the anger out of them, and they all murmured their love for him in return. Collin could see the sadness in Ozaki and tried to cheer him up,

"Well Uncle Ozaki," he announced, "I should be the one thanking you! This experience has made me a better man." He looked at William, "And you Uncle Will; you have brought me a peace I thought I would never know. Thank you!"

William looked down at Dana who looked up at him with a big smile. "I think we all found something special this Christmas." Collin and Catherine stepped forward and threw their arms around the entire group, open joy surrounding them. After a moment, William broke off and faced his valet.

"We did it, old friend! Your honor is intact!"

Only a small sad smile cracked Osaki's veneer. "Perhaps it is, my friend. Only you could have pulled it off." He bowed deeply. "You are the greatest of all."

William blushed at the unusual display of affection. "We all did it! Together...as a family!"

Ozaki nodded sadly. "I wish I could stay and celebrate with you but forgive me, I must return to my home." He looked straight at William. "Tonight...tonight I must be Japanese."

Disappointment washed across William's face, but he stood and struck a regal pose. We will miss your company tonight old friend, but we understand.

Do what you must. You will come up in the morning, won't you?"

"Of course. Good night then." He turned to leave, then stopped and said loudly. "Merry Christmas to you all!"

As soon as they heard the door shut, Collin asked William, "What gives with him Uncle Will? I thought he'd be gloating over how we pulled this off!"

William took a sip of his chocolate and frowned. Suddenly, his jaw dropped and he said, "Oh, my Lord! I just remembered something I read last month. It was in a story the Times ran about the gift of the cherry trees in Washington. The name of the Japanese ambassador was Yoshi Ozaki! He must be Ozaki's father..."

They were all stunned into silence. Dana finally said, "That must be why Yukio wanted Ozaki to return to Washington with him? Yukio asked him after he read the telegram."

Collin wanted to chase Ozaki out the door and talk some sense into him. He would have given anything to see his father one last time. "Why...Why did he refuse?"

William sighed. "I don't know the whole story. He never told and I never asked. All I do know is that when Ozaki was a young man, he committed some...bad act, for which his father banished him from Japan to America. He never had contact with him again, at least, not to my knowledge."

"Still," Collin insisted, "It's his father!"

William looked him straight in the eye. "Yes, and it's his business. We must let him deal with this in his own fashion. Consider it the last act of our little play!" William looked at them all sternly, "You must not let Ozaki know we figured it out. The Japanese deal with these things differently than us westerners! I'm counting on your discretion."

They all nodded their assent, and then Collin clapped his hands together. "Well, if there's nothing to do about it, no sense in the rest of us moping around! It's Christmas Eve! I say we decorate the tree, have a little supper, and then head off to midnight mass! What do you say?"

William was overjoyed to hear Collin suggest they go to church. "Absolutely! That sounds like a wonderful evening!" He beamed and added, "I take it you had a good talk with Miss Joilet today?"

Collin nodded and smiled at Catherine. "She made a lot of things clear to me. I'll tell you all about it later." Collin clapped his hands together. "Great! Just let Catherine and I go to the Aunt Polly and change and we'll be back to get started."

After they left, Dana and William sat and sipped their chocolate. Things were suddenly serene, and they enjoyed sharing the moment. Dana sighed and stood up. "I suppose I should dig the Christmas decorations out of the storage room and think about starting supper. Is there something you would prefer, Mr. Gillette?"

William reached out with a hand and pulled her back into her seat. "It's still William and Dana."

"I thought you said it was the last act?"

William stared down his nose at her, "I'm the director and I say when this play is over! Also, you will not need to prepare dinner. We will dine at the Inn tonight. From there we can go to mass. Lastly, you shall sit and finish your chocolate with me, and after, we will both dig out the ornaments!"

Dana's smile was polite, but her eyes were lit with joy. "My, My! Do you have any more surprises for me?"

He grinned and pointed upwards. Suspended from the ceiling above them was a sprig of mistletoe...

22

    Collin and Catherine returned within an hour and William opened a bottle of champagne to toast the holiday. Then they dove into the boxes of Christmas ornaments and soon the tree was draped with garland, hung with glass bulbs, and painted pinecones. Everyone held their breath when Collin pulled out an ornament that his father had given William years before, afraid it might set off one of his tirades, but Collin just smiled at it fondly for a moment then placed it on the tree. Soon the great room looked festive enough to begin their celebration of the Yule.

    William and Dana freshened up and with Catherine and Collin, they went off to enjoy a fine dinner at the Inn in town. They feasted on baked ham and yams, followed by a bread pudding with a rich bourbon sauce for dessert.

    William patted his lips clean with a napkin and announced. "That was superb! Jimmy out did himself tonight!"

    Catherine gave him a sly look and said, "Perhaps, someday, you'll need to find a replacement for Dana. Maybe you could lure him away."

    Collin was confused by the comment, but William ignored it and Dana gave her a look that screamed 'Drop it!' Before he could ask what she meant, Chief Inspector Rowan came up to the table.

    "Well, well, the notorious Gillette gang! Where's your boss?"

William smiled. "He lost his new position when his brother left! By the way, I wish to thank you for playing along with us."

Rowan shrugged. "No skin off my neck. Happy to oblige. So, what was up? Are you planning on bringing Boxing Day to America like you did Sherlock Holmes?"

"Just this once, I think." William replied.

"Well, I'd still love to hear the story, but tonight I have to get home to my wife and kids. Have to make sure Santa comes after the kids are asleep!"

William stood and put out his hand. "Give our love to Martha, Brett, and baby Isabella. We wish you a very Merry Christmas, Kevin."

Rowan took his hand and held it. "Merry Christmas William." He looked around the table. "To all of you."

The hours had passed quickly by then and it was time to head off to the church.

"I hope I'm welcome.", Collin said to William sheepishly. "I haven't been exactly cordial to God this past year."

William chuckled. "Don't fret about it Collin. You were angry- not evil! I'm sure God knows the difference."

William woke after nine Christmas morning, early for getting in bed after midnight Christmas Eve mass. He stirred during the night thinking about Osaki. Today everything would be right with his world, except he ached for the pain Osaki must have felt for his father's illness and the hasty departure of his brother Yukio. Still, Ozaki made it clear he wanted to grieve in the Japanese way, and he found the strength within his heart to accept this. He also knew the others would be gathering soon. He dressed and groomed himself, then lurked just inside his bedroom door that was slightly ajar.

He kept an eye on the mirror he had strategically place in the hallway. He could see that it had snowed and the view outside the windows was crisp and bright with sunshine. Patiently, he waited until Dana stepped into the hallway, heading for the stairs. She was looking down at the great room when she was startled by William stepping beside her.

"Merry Christmas, Dana" he held out his arm, "May I escort you to coffee?"

She arched an eyebrow at him. "That depends. Are you going to put me under the mistletoe again?"

William reddened and sputtered, "No, no... well...I wasn't...I wouldn't...I was only thinking of coffee!"

"Well...alright," she took his arm. "I will accept your offer kind sir. Merry Christmas."

They hadn't gotten to the bottom of the stairs when they heard the front door open up and Collin and Catherine charged into the room, arms full of wrapped boxes, and Collin crying out "Merry Christmas! The Clauses are here!"

The couples greeted and hugged, and then Dana suggested they head to the kitchen and make coffee after placing the presents under the tree. They stopped in surprise when they reached the dining room.

The table was set for breakfast, with carafes of coffee and plates of bagels and pastries. The table was decorated with garland and a large poinsettia graced the middle. Ozaki stood next to the table, back in his house uniform. He bowed deeply.

"Merry Christmas everyone! Please, sit! I will serve the coffee." He smiled at them, with love in his eyes.

Stunned, they greeted him and did as he asked. William smiled contentedly. Everything was as it should be.

After breakfast, they headed for the tree to open presents. On the way, William looked at his valet and said sternly. "You get a pass on Christmas Ozaki, but you and I will discuss the...gift of my Winslow to your brother."

"Please let me honor you with a Christmas gift prior to our discussion." Ozaki replied. He went behind the couch and pulled out a large flat rectangular package. William tore the wrapping off where he stood.

It was a painting of a fisherman, pulling in his nets from a dory under a dark and forbidding sky. It was in the same style as the picture Ozaki gifted to his brother, but of a different subject. In the corner was a familiar signature. Winslow Homer.

William stared at the picture with watery eyes, flabbergasted that Ozaki had procured two masterpieces William was touched that Ozaki had been planning this Christmas present for so long.

Ozaki looked up at him and deadpanned, "Having two would have been...ostentatious!" With that, he walked on.

William set the painting down carefully on the couch then joined the others at the base of the tree, just in time to hear Catherine say, "Quiet – what is that sound coming from the rear of the tree?"

Collin looked at his uncle slyly. "I guess we'll need to put it to Sherlock! Maybe he can solve the mystery!"

"Perhaps he can." William murmured and held up a hand for silence. He cocked his head, then walked around the back of the tree, and lifted a lower branch. He smiled and gestured for the rest of them to join him.

They all gathered to look past him at a pile of material, formed into a nest. Inside the mound, was a mother cat, lying on her side with a new born meowing litter vying for their mother's milk? They noticed the material that was cradling them and laughed with joy.

Among some bits of cloth was a glove, an oven mitt, a pair of men's underwear and a knit hat. Also visible was a white swath of fine silk, decorated by graceful blue herons. Collin laughed loudly. "Looks like the dragon lady slapped the wrong cat!"

Catherine swatted Collin on the arm and William smiled at the tiny kittens like a proud father and especially proud of the nest mama cat had built. "I think it's nice to have some new borns around on Christmas!"

Catherine smiled coyly and said, "You will have one more by next year."

William, Dana, and Ozaki's eyes flew open wide, and smiles broke out all around. It took a Collin a moment longer for it to sink in, and then his face lit up with joy and threw his arms around

Catherine. William cried out. "Oh, my!" and pulled Dana to his chest and kissed her soundly."

When Dana looked up, the other three were watching them with various looks of surprise on their faces.

William dropped his arms and stammered, "I mean...that's wonderful news!

Later on, after the Christmas feast, Collin and William stepped out onto the veranda. The river below was a dark swath that was accented the pristine whiteness of the fresh snow. On the horizon, the sky glowed with the colors of the rainbow as the sun slowly set. Lighting a cigar, Collin looked up at William.

"Well Uncle Will, you were right as always. This is the one Christmas I shall never forget!"

The End
Jimmy Bennett
11/24/21

Biography

Jimmy Bennett has been a professional chef for forty years, proudly serving the residents and tourist around Mystic, Connecticut.

His love of the New England coastline, local history, and mystery classics has inspired him to write several William Gillette – Sherlock Holmes mysteries.

Jimmy has been creating books set along the Connecticut shoreline since 1998, and lives in Mystic, Connecticut.

Books Published by Jimmy Bennett

The Case of the Flying Corpse

The Case of the Floating Corpse

**Accounts of William Gillette
Five Mysteries**

Jimmy's books are available at local Connecticut and Rhode Island Book Stores and Amazon.com

Made in the USA
Monee, IL
17 May 2024

58329836R10109